# FORGED IN FIRE
# —THE LONGSTREET—
# Family and Fights

## Volume 2

## MICHAEL MASSA

Published by:
R.H. Publishing
3411 Preston Rd. Ste C-146
Frisco, Texas 75034

Copyright © 2020, Michael Massa

ISBN#978-1-945693-59-5

Unless noted, all Scripture quotations are from THE NEW KING JAMES VERSION (NKJV). © 1982 by Thomas Nelson, Inc. Used by permission. All rights reserved.

*Even though the names in the story often reflect some of the names of my family, there is no negative connection between each of them and the characters portrayed in this story. On the contrary, any positives are intentionally accurate.

"How great is Your goodness,
which You have hidden for Your fearers;
You have worked for those who trust in You
before the sons of mankind.
You shall hide them in the secrecy
of Your presence from the plots of man;
You shall cover them in a booth
from the strife of tongues …"
(Psalm 31:19-21).

# DEDICATION

This book is dedicated to the servants the Lord has often used to hone and sharpen my life. The list is far too long to give here, but I am grateful to the Lord for each of them ... the Sunday School teachers, the intercessors, and the leaders who granted me favor. All of them have been used to weave into my heart and life, a tapestry of diligence, focus, priorities, and discipline. Though I have not always cooperated at the level they supplied these things, I am grateful for the multitude the Lord has sent.

Always at the front of that list are my parents from the beginning and then later my wife, Nancy—I am much less without their contributions.

# TABLE OF CONTENTS

# INTRODUCTION

King Egbert had whispered the secret into Mark's ear. In his lifetime Mark could voice the secret only one time. That one time would be directly into the ear of the governor of Essex, and no one else could hear it.

Mark accomplished his royal task with the supernatural help of the King of all kings, the prayers of his family and King Egbert, along with the help of his stalwart covenant keeping friends, Galvin and Edward. These two fellow-warriors had been sent with Mark on the mission.

The secret King Egbert whispered into Mark's ear, which Mark had whispered into the governor's ear, was this: Egbert's father, King Wilford, had understood the strategic wisdom of spreading supplies, positioned in hidden locations, throughout the realm. These hidden stashes could be used in any crisis and would provide benefits quickly since they would be closer to any point of need.

The idea was excellent, but it required the highest degree of secrecy to be effective. This massive undertaking required more than two years to prepare and 18 months to fulfill. The king and his son set out to construct and then implement the plan. Places were chosen by dividing the nation into a geographic grid that provided seclusion and accessibility. People were chosen to receive, store and guard these supplies. Those who were entrusted with that responsibility were of the highest character. An extensive and stringent evaluation was carried out to verify their trustworthiness. It was only after they had been thoroughly validated that they could be informed of the importance of the assignment.

Still, they would not be told all the details. The selection of the right individuals and families was crucial to the plan's success. They found many sincere people, but the truly trustworthy were few. There must be no question as to their loyalty to the king and his purpose. There was two years of active searching and validation before all the people and locations were secured. After that, the provisions were gathered and placed.

The secret storage areas included farms, holes in the sides of hills and even an old, abandoned mill that had been demolished by a storm. That old mill was hidden on the back edges of a faithful farmer's land, and it was considered too dangerous to enter, lest it fall apart. The king's carpenters reinforced weakened points with old but stable beams. Those hidden supports sustained the perception that the mill was unsafe to enter. It was a perfect site.

Those storage areas had to be restocked systematically. The maintenance and ongoing security of the plan was an enhanced challenge because the restocking had to be done during the nighttime for three of the sites. The process revealed how kings come to greatly honor anyone who proves they are faithful. Few knew the full extent of the project, and it was essential that no one, especially the realm's enemies, would ever know of the strategy or the locations.

These storage areas must be guarded by people and families who would lay their life down for the king without hesitation.

Still, because of the reality and impact of generational changes, the king was specifically on the lookout for fathers who raised faithful children and grandchildren. Such a forceful requirement reduced even more the number who could be qualified. The King had been searching for families with long-term character and strength. Strong nations are established on such households.

In collaboration with his son, King Wilford established seven places where they concealed and stored these supplies. The items they stored included such things as preserved-in-salt meat, sealed grains, weapons of all kinds, oil, seeds, silver, blankets, maps, farming tools and the kind of things necessary to respond to a crisis. There were also directions on how the supplies were to be distributed.

The effort was an overwhelming task and involved multitudinous details. Egbert had learned much in the furnace of secrecy, which had been forced on him by his father's rare wisdom. He was reminded of God's revelation to Joseph in Egypt in the Book of Genesis. That story of Joseph's wisdom to store up grain for the coming famine, had inspired him to accomplish his task with excellence. As father and son, the two kings had been storing and maintaining these sites for 20 years. Egbert created two additional locations after his father's death. These two new sites were inside caves on royal land.

After Mark heard the secret, he went on an epic journey through enemy-occupied territory to speak the secret one time to the governor. He was astonished at the abundance prepared by the king for a crisis. The location was not far from the governor's own land. He gave thanks to the true heavenly King for his earthly king's wisdom.

Mark, Galvin, and Edward took the governor's most trusted servant to the secret supply site. There, Mark used a code word with the nondescript farmer upon whose land the supplies were hidden. The farmer did not know how much was hidden or why the king had hidden it, but he had sworn to dedicate his family to the sacred trust of guarding what the king had placed there. This was, after all, a royal assignment. He knew it was always an honor to be faithful to any responsibility the king gives, whether he accesses you or not. The farmer fulfilled his mission in obscurity. None of the neighbors or his extended family knew anything about it. Faithfulness to the assignment was what counted. The king's purpose cannot advance without the loyal maturity of his servants.

King Egbert had given Mark the details of the location, what was stored there, how the governor could use it and how Mark and his team were to initially oversee the distribution of the supplies. As the king anticipated, these resources provided more than enough support for the victory, and the governor found unexpected treasures. These unanticipated benefits included three Longstreet swords.

After that, Mark, Galvin, and Edward returned to King Egbert with diligent intention. Galvin and Edward had seen the hidden supplies. They did not understand how or why they had been hidden.

Mark did not explain what he knew.

He had too much honor to tell them … ever.

His friends did not ask. They had too much honor to ask … ever.

They did not speak of what they had seen to anyone ... ever. Each of them had too much honor to do that ... ever.

Mark reported to the king shortly after arriving home. He had first gone to greet Susanna. When he had quickly freshened up, he made his way to the castle. He was ushered into the throne room as if he was a guest monarch. The king stood to welcome him, stepped down from the throne platform and embraced Mark in front of the those assembled in the court.

Mark was surprised by the royal approval and the embrace. He had never heard of the king standing for anyone. Mark briefly whispered into Egbert's ear the report and promised a full written account the next day. With great exuberance, the king announced his favor toward Mark for the courage and valor he and his friends had displayed.

A royal decree was written and presented in a public ceremony a week later. Each of the trio of loyal friends was honored specifically, but Mark was singled out as the leader of this epic and unexplained task. He was presented with a ruby-jeweled ring and given the title *'friend of the king'* for his loyal and sacrificial service. The crowd cheered in agreement.

The honor was a blessing, but with that word of approval, Mark's heart unwittingly allowed a subtle seed of self-importance *and pride* to be planted. That seed would grow unrecognized, until a moment of crisis that would propel him to death's door.

# Chapter One

# BAAL'S BOY

King David, of the Bible, gave a warning to future leaders about the sons of Baal in his final words, recorded in 2 Samuel 23:6, 7,

> "But *the sons* of rebellion (Baal) *shall all* be as thorns thrust away because they cannot be taken with hands. But the man who touches them must be armed (filled) with iron and the shaft of a spear, and they shall be utterly burned with fire in their place."

When the Bible speaks of wicked people or evil men, they are frequently termed sons of Belial or sons of Baal. This term is used in the Old Covenant to describe rebels and idol worshipers. The New Covenant also includes warnings about them. They are most often men of overt selfishness. They can be loyal to an idol or themselves, but they are never loyal to the Lord. They are perversely stubborn and often produce much grief.

As the verse expresses, you cannot overcome these Baal boys effectively, unless you are filled with iron and the shaft of a spear. There are few who can rightly deal with them, because of the processes that God uses to fill someone with divine iron. That road is not easy and most who are invited by the Lord into the rigors of that goal falter. Mark was on the path of being filled with this holy iron, but he did not always respond rightly to the pressures. No one does.

Mark would have six sons of Belial in his life, but Erik would be the worst.

Mark met Erik as an adversary several times after their first encounter, and they engaged in severe fights three times. Each fight would cost more than the one before. The last one was incomprehensible for both!

The first time they met was not a fight and it took place a few months after Mark and his family moved to the castle grounds to serve the king.

Erik was angrily rushing through the crowded market outside the castle with no concern for anyone else. He was embarrassed and angry. He was furious with her! She had rejected him. She had slapped him … so hard that his left ear was soundless and one of his teeth was loosened.

All he had tried to do was kiss her. He had already given her flowers, and she refused them. Then, he gave her a hand-woven necklace with shiny stones beaded on a string. She refused that too. He wanted her to like him … she was beautiful. Lastly, he had pressed her into an embrace, without her cooperation. As he leaned in for the kiss, she squirmed away. Without thinking and with some irritation, he impulsively grabbed her. He was forcing her lips to his when she moved like a mountain cat and swung an open hand hard against his face and ear. He lost his hearing on that side. She ran toward her friends. Erik stared with fiery eyes as she fled.

*"I will be back to get my kiss, whether you want it or not,"* he thought. *"You think you are too good for me? You will find out, young lady, I am not the quitting kind. I will get you back or no one will have you!"*

Erik was fuming over her rejection of him. He was tired of it. Rejection was all he had ever known. The agony started with his dad's drunken-fueled and anger-filled beatings—those had been a furnace of repeated pain and violence. That historic brutality formed him into a hardened man, but he did not have the kind of masculinity that served others. Injustice applied with harsh hands often creates perverse reasonings in a mind. The brain becomes twisted, and that person does not rightly see themselves, others, or God.

> Injustice applied with harsh hands often creates perverse reasonings in a mind.

This current pain was just one more wounding wrong added to his story. The lady's speedy slap penetrated him deeply. But Erik was the sort of man who could not see that some of the blame for the pain in his life was not there because of others. He should take responsibility for his actions, not blame them. He had become a man who was rarely humble enough to yield to instruction. His unrestrained anger would ruin his life, and it would add severe consequences to many people, including Mark and Susanna.

Moving quickly now, Erik was filled with a boiling rage, barely capped by the smallest degree of self-awareness. He did not really care who he might jostle or push aside as he pressed through the crowd. With his heart set on his anger, Erik did not see Mark standing on the crowded trajectory of his accelerating pace. He had turned to look again, one last time toward the girl, when in that precise moment, he was halted as he crushed into Mark's back. But Erik was not just stopped, he was repelled backwards. He felt as though he had run into a tree. Mark had not moved. Erik was not as large as Mark, but he was still a strong-bodied fellow, and this wall-of-a-man had arrested his angry track. Erik was stunned. Everyone else he had bumped into had moved away or fallen. Erik brooded over this strong man, *"Who is this guy?"*

Mark turned and said, "I am sorry, sir, I did not see you." Erik was mad and hurting and embarrassed that a girl hit him so hard. He had no care for this big guy blocking his path. He looked up at the giant—grunted, growled, and moved on.

Unknown to either of them at that time, Mark and Erik would run into one another again and again. This first meeting was unexpected, all the others would be dangerous and life changing. Erik would change the future for both. Two extremes would be generated. The wounds … unimaginable.

# Chapter Two

# BANDITS

"You shall not follow a crowd to do evil,"
(Exodus 23:2).

In the first years of their marriage, Mark and Susanna merged into a wonder-filled unity. The days at the castle were full of joy, and the privilege of serving under a righteous king created a freedom from the common aggravations and disorder selfish leaders can plant in their subjects. Most do not comprehend the degree of force that leadership exerts in positive or negative impacts on the ones they govern. But even the not-so-loyal-of-heart followers can be blessed by righteous kings, and righteous citizens are often 'burdened' by ungodly rulers.

Societies, which have ungodly rulers, are more prone to generate surly characters, but even the best of leaders can be taxed by the development of those with lazy and self-absorbed viewpoints. No culture is exempted from them. Jesus explained how in the Kingdom of God there are "wheat and tares" (sons of God and sons of the evil one). Ungodly rulers are a challenge to walk and work with. And God uses that challenge to form His character in the faithful.

Early in Mark's training with the Blue Guard, the king

had given a task to him. It was the first assignment for Mark specifically directed by the king since his initial success against the Berserker raid with Sir John. This first assignment was long before he made the trip to the Governor of Essex and the secret storage areas. He had been entrusted with some information, along with a gift the king wanted to give to a friend in an area west and south of the castle. Mark had to go to a part of the nation he had not often traveled entered. He was not concerned.

Sir Mark had requested the King's permission for Susanna to go with him. It was a non-military action through the heart of the King's territory. The journey would be less than four hours one way, and his request was granted. Susanna went with him. They left early to arrive before noon. They used one of the king's wagons and Mark was thrilled Susanna could come along. Later, he realized just how important it was that she had come. If she had not, someone would have died. As for Susanna, she simply needed a rest from her daily chores. And Mark really wanted the time alone with her. They were looking forward to a good and glad day. Neither of them could have known how difficult and how wonderful the day would become.

The trip itself was delightful; the weather was splendid. The sky was majestic with billowing clouds, fresh breezes and as they traveled, the mysterious and often unnoticed songs of birds melodied the journey. The birds were choreographing the trip with their musical accompaniment. They had lunch with the king's friend and prepared to return after a brief walk around the man's farm. The king's friend also had gifts for the king. He gave Mark two large parcels for presentation to Egbert as thanks for the gracious gift the king provided. Mark and another man carried the two heavy boxes into the back of the wagon and covered them with a thick brown blanket. They bid the man farewell and were off.

The prettiest part of the return was over a treeless ridge descending into a verdant valley with a stream paralleling the road for over a mile. Elm, Oak and Ash trees stood as natural pillars adorning the terrain. Mark and Susanna felt compelled to stop and simply take in the view. With his back turned, Mark was stepping off the wagon to help Susanna down, when suddenly eight men surrounded them. They had been lying in wait with evil intent a few feet away behind some large oak trees. Each carried a knife and two wielded swords. The leader spoke with a strong degree of brutish confidence, "You can leave the lady and get those things out from under the blanket. Do it now!"

Mark was not an impatient man, but this young leader was pushing hard with his tone. A gang of young men can be more dangerous than they recognize. A fool may act like a fool without understanding the wrongness of his behavior. Although fools may be sincerely ignorant, that lack of understanding does not exempt them from the consequences of their wrongs. And they can still generate severe damage. Often, there are no ethical limits to their behavior, not

> Although fools may be sincerely ignorant, that lack of understanding does not exempt them from the consequences of their wrongs.

because they are rooted into evil, but because they are unaware of the doors opened by silly decisions. This type of gang action is prohibited in the Word of God. Unchecked, these kinds of efforts can ruin their lives, but they were in no mood to hear righteous instruction.

Mark cooperated in unloading the wagon, but the boxes were bulky. Although his strength was great, they were hard to unload without help. He finally got them off the wagon and realized the thieves had no way to carry them anywhere. But that insight had not dawned on them.

The lead guy spoke again, "Step away from the lady and stand over there."

Mark smiled. These young ruffians were clueless about the extent of the capabilities of the large man they were addressing. With a calm demeanor, he replied, "Sir, you do not understand. I made a covenant before God to that beautiful lady there," as he pointed at Susanna. "My vow was committed to her in the presence of the Most Holy God of heaven. I promised her and Him I would love, honor, and protect her for the rest of my life. I will never leave her. I will never do that. You would have to kill me to get to her." Susanna smiled easily at his loyalty. She was not afraid nor was he. His comment was not a threat or some silly attempt at bravado. It was the truth. He would not leave her to them. He said the words casually, with an unwavering resolve.

The eight laughed at the 'religious' tone of his words and perceived the formality of Mark's confession as a facade. They had grown up in homes where 'church-words' were a cover for hypocrisy. They did not know, nor had they seen the reality and substance formed in a life that was genuinely given to the Lord.

Mark knew there would be a fight. The only question now was how many of them he would have to incapacitate to cause the others to back down. He was already planning the first three moves to take out the two who had swords. But that would not be enough. He would have to stop at least two others. Then the rest would run away. Many such gangs are often made up of fearful ones who are filled with so much pain they must hide the fear of being hurt further with violent behavior.

The first man, the leader, was indeed such a man, and he was able to use the sword. Mark knew that inherently; he saw how easily he wielded his sword. The way he held it indicated a strong acquaintance with its use. Mark's first action would be against him. Mark was internally positioning to implement his strategy …

Then, without warning and in a firm, yet feminine voice, Susanna spoke. She was interrupting Mark's internal strategizing with a surprising exactness of speech. She spoke as if she was the older sister of these young men.

Susanna stood and said, "Gentlemen, my husband is a member of the king's Royal Blue Guard. He has fought against Viking Berserkers when he was outnumbered 10 to one, when all of them had swords. He killed them all without wounds to his body. He is one of the best warriors in the realm. He is not afraid of you. You, however, should be afraid of him. The wisest thing you can do is to lay down your weapons, and then put the gifts intended for King Egbert back in the king's wagon, so my husband can give a good report to the king about your service."

She spoke with a matter-of-fact tone and with no pretense,

no fear. She spoke the truth.

Now, all these young men had been rebuked before … but none of them had ever seen a husband stand with and for his wife, nor had any of them ever been called 'gentlemen.' None of them had been rebuked with any hope implied in the rebuke … 'so my husband can give a good report to the king about your service.' It was a moment of strangeness for them. They could not say it, but they felt loved as Susanna spoke, and this being cared for kind of 'parental peace' settled into them. They somehow felt 'respected' in her speech. Her words had turned off the angry fire in them. As if a new day was starting, they saw themselves and their foolishness for the first time, and yet, they were received, not rejected.

Mark had a faint grin on his face. He was impressed with his wife. Mark raised his right hand with the seal of the king on the ruby ring he wore. He began to lower his sword before the eight lowered their weapons. They could not escape the simple force of her words. They were humbled and unified rather quickly. Lowering their weapons to the ground, they immediately began to lift the large boxes back into the wagon.

What had been intended as a brief stop for Mark and Susanna, was transformed into a three-hour mentoring session with eight young men who had been isolated by frustrations and internal bruises. Mark and Susanna counseled them as an older brother and sister might. They ended up confessing their wrongs toward Mark and Susanna, listening together and then laughing as a family would. This man and his wife had shown them genuine care and respect—a new experience for each of them.

These eight young men were accepted by this formal couple who had a living reality of loyalty to the Lord inside. The impact was real. Three of those eight would join the king's army and were trained by Mark in the use of swords. Two others became god-fearing merchants, and the other three all became solid citizens and parents in the years ahead.

Mark spoke to Susanna on the way home. "You and I make a good team. You were quite wise back there. I always knew you as a perceptive lady, but you took an adversarial moment and turned it to reconciliation and friendship. You are an excellent peacemaker. I am impressed. Thank you for the lesson. I should remember that." (Indeed, he should have …)

# Chapter Three

# PICNIC BEARS

You don't want to meet a bear robbed of her cubs!

Mark and Susanna would ultimately live into their 80s and become great-grandparents with a marvelous tribe of young men and women as a legacy surrounding them. The family would spread out into the realm of the king for generations to come. Yet, the story of their life together was not only about the good things they experienced. The trails and trials of their days included the many struggles they overcame before their long-life together was fulfilled. Some old pains returned with new strength, and a new and powerful enemy was revealed. Before Mark's life was over, he would face obstacles he had never imagined. The family did not come through these oppositions unscathed. Scars were formed that Mark could never erase from his memory or his body.

The words of Matthew's Gospel describe the Kingdom of God as wheat and tares growing up in a field. The wheat represents the sons of the Kingdom of God, and the tares are the sons of the wicked one. Both Mark and Susanna would have to reckon with those sons of Baal up close and in a deeply personal fashion. Both would be dealt with by the Lord regarding the stubborn, prideful, and selfish ways in their hearts too. The battles were spiritual, emotional, and physical. The process was demanding and taxed them at deeply intimate levels.

The Lord seeks to validate His claim and His name on those who follow Him. For those who say they are Christ's followers, that confession is meaningless if it is never tested and verified. Anyone can advocate loyalty to the Lord during the springtime when the flowers are fragrant and the breezes are mild, but will they release His character when life's unjust storms rage and carnal urges are surging? That question must be faced for every true disciple.

> Anyone can advocate loyalty to the Lord during the springtime when the flowers are fragrant and the breezes are mild, but will they release His character when life's unjust storms rage and carnal urges are surging?

Mark and Susanna were placed in several testing places. Mark did not always score well, and one of these tests would bring him to his knees before God and others. Many disciples do not continue to submit to the transforming pressures the Lord uses during our life. But Mark was committed from early in his life to submit to Him, and the Lord kept on hammering the impurities out.

One Sunday, a monk from the monastery had come to the church's gathering. His message was describing the character of "sluggards." He said that sluggards could be motivated by witchcraft. When the congregation heard that word, they winced internally and some with confusion whispered audibly, "Witchcraft?"

He explained that one of the original words for witchcraft was *perierga* and could mean "the desire to go around the work." He described refusing to exert the necessary effort, and yet, still be expecting the benefits from having worked, as a resistance to God's ways and an attribute of those who move in the fruit of the fleshly nature. The New Testament Book of Galatians calls this witchcraft.

The monk explained that the idea *perierga* generates a mindset where we think we can gain the fruit of working without investing the time to plow, sow, water and then reap the harvest. Such a mindset causes a person to become guilty of "magical" thinking, as if they could make some benefit appear out of nothing, like receiving a harvest with no labor. That sermon had lodged in Mark's heart and mind, partially due to the way the monk had proclaimed it.

> "You will have a job in heaven! The Lord did not curse work! He cursed the ground because of Adam and Eve's unbelieving disobedience!"

The monk lifted his voice and shouted, "God designed us to work!" It was a rare display of emotion, and he continued with an enthusiastic proclamation, "You will have a job in heaven! The Lord did not curse work! He cursed the ground because of Adam and Eve's unbelieving disobedience!"

The Longstreet family knew about hard work and honor and faith in the God Who created everything. Mark remembered the conversation around the meal after church that day, as the family discussed the force of the monk's message, and the strength necessary to avoid that 'witchcraft' thinking process. So, concerning the carnal sin of witchcraft, which yearned for fruit without working—that kind of iniquity was not allowed near the Longstreet house.

There are truly wicked people who are consciously and overtly devilish in motive. Truly wicked people think it is good to make other people pay for the wrongs the wicked people themselves have done. They have a perversely stubborn and consciously rebellious mind. They oppose anything truly worthwhile. For them, it is sport to do evil, and to ruin something beautiful is a pleasure. They delight in twisting circumstances into ugly, chaotic moments to match the misery of their own heart. To recognize these kinds of extremes, which can be generated from a vehement antagonism can be confusing and heart-breaking, but wise warriors are not paralyzed by their disorder.

> They delight in twisting circumstances into ugly, chaotic moments to match the misery of their own heart.

The selfish commitments wicked people are often rooted in some harsh personal history and open doors in the soul to demonic forces, often unwittingly. People don't want to acknowledge this prospect. But saying that an evil person only has mental problems, cannot fully explain the degree of dark and perverse capacities that can be expressed from evil spiritual forces.

The Longstreet family was not wicked. They lived in a house of peace. Many families do not know what it means to live in peace. They may have the finest things the world has to offer, but there is hell in their home. This was not the case for Mark and Susanna. With five children, born over a 14-year span, (three boys, then two girls), they grew into a closely knit bunch, and the children developed into the maturity their parents had grown up with.

Sure, there were the usual spats and bickering all children engage in, but the mealtimes were especially delightful and often lasted longer because they loved to be together. Aaron, Christopher, Zechariah, then Jennifer and Michaela were a special quintet that blended Mark and Susanna's traits, both physically and spiritually. Each child was uniquely gifted, but they all carried the stamp of strength and stability in which their parents moved. The home was a fortress of life and love and courage.

They lived in the house the king provided for Mark and his parents when the king enlisted him to join the Royal Blue Guard. Though their home was stable, the struggles and near-death experiences still came—several times.

Once, when Mark was free of his duties, he and Susanna had journeyed away from the castle to spend a day together on a picnic. They were separated from all the pressures and responsibilities of the king's court. They expected a different kind of day ... and they got it.

They had pre-planned the trip and Mark's responsibilities had been given to other trusted men of the guard. Strongly in love, they had been anticipating this picnic day. They took the family wagon several miles north to a valley James had discovered the year before. It was nestled between five tree-quilted hills with

31

a deep blue lake, fed by the runoff of the mountain snows. The lake's water was clear and cold. The bottom was easily visible even though James estimated it was 30 feet deep.

The day was fresh. It was laced with peaceful sharing, laughter, and listening to the breezes blow. The intimate conversations about dreams and hopes for them and their as-yet-future children filled the day with glad expectations as they sat side by side. Hugs and tender kisses had been exchanged. The sky was a dusty blue with a crisp breeze and the day held the residual tinges of winter. Mark was glad since Susanna was prone to snuggle even more than normal when it was cooler.

After the picnic meal, while lying on the blanket, an unanticipated guest arrived. A bear cub, ambling up from a stream-filled ravine that was created by the lake's overflow, approached their picnic site. They were downwind, so they saw the cub before the cub smelled them. But Mark and Susanna instinctively knew a very real threat would come with that cub. *Where was Momma?*

Bears were rarely seen in this part of the nation, though some occasionally wandered south from the Scot's lands. Mark and Susanna stood up slowly as the cub approached. The baby bear still had not yet seen or smelled them and remained unaware that its meandering course brought them an increasing risk of Momma's forceful defense of her cub. Mark and Susanna knew she would not be far away. Just then, they saw Momma approach with her broad, dark back easing over the hill's border. She was a large brown bear and guarding her cub was all she lived for.

Momma rounded the hill's edge; she saw her cub and then

sniffed the air. Her more mature nose smelled the aroma of 'other' before she saw Mark and Susanna.

Mark angled in front of Susanna; there was no hint of fear in either of them. They were alert and ready, though neither knew exactly what they would or should do. Mark whispered, "Slowly take the oak stick we used to cook the meat. Use it if you need to."

She knelt casually and picked up the stick as if she had done it 1,000 times before. Mark yearned for the Longstreet, (his home-forged sword), which he had left at home. This first lesson of the day was something he must never repeat. He should not have left his sword at home. Every warrior always has his weapon. That had been a standing order from his mentor, Sir John. In the training, he had constantly drilled into them, "You are always a warrior for the king; there is never a time when you are to be without your weapon!" But Mark had to come back to the present. He would reckon with correcting himself for his lapse in discipline later.

> "You are always a warrior for the king; there is never a time when you are to be without your weapon!"

The closest tree was too far to run for; both bears stood between them and that tree. The first limbs were too high to climb, and Mark knew that bears could climb trees with an unimaginable speed. His grandfather told him, 'You have no idea how fast a bear can climb a tree … I saw one do it once; it was breath-taking." *Forget the tree.*

This bear and cub were now less than 100 feet away. The

two bears had come up unnoticed in the shallow ravine with a rocky creek surging through its banks. The noise of rushing water had been a wonderful backdrop for their picnic, but it had concealed the bears' approach (a second lesson to remember).

Momma growled. The cub stopped … looked up and saw them for the first time. All four of them were still. The wind stilled too. Silence came—for less than three seconds—though it felt like a minute. The cub was ignorant of the violent prospects of this encounter. The other three were not.

Mark was intent on protecting his bride and getting these bears away. He was not afraid of the momma bear, *"Hadn't I raced through those Berserkers?"* He was startled by the arrogant thought. *"Who do you think you are? When did you become a woodsman with skills to surpass this wild beast? That pride must be dealt with too"* (a third lesson, no doubt). But the bear was there, so he laid his pride-problem down—*just for a moment.* He had a bear to beat and a bride to bless. But Momma was only intent on protecting her cub and getting the others away.

> He had a bear to beat and a bride to bless.

Then, the story of King David killing the lion and the bear flashed through his mind, and Mark calmed a bit. He set his eyes intently on Momma. He crouched slightly, ready to act. Then he whispered to Susanna, "Go straight at the cub with the stick, but only after I charge the momma."

With no warning and not wanting the bear to dictate the timing, Mark sprang forward, his form fully extended, shouting like a wild man. The next scenes, totaling less than a minute in duration, unfolded rapidly, but each act was distinct and separately memorable as it sequenced:

- The large man leaped forward and charged the momma bear like a maniac—yelling full-throated,

- Susanna delayed for an instant, since she was startled by her man's explosive action.

- The cub froze, also startled by the man's display.

- Momma stood upright immediately, unafraid and concerned only with her cub. She was not intimidated by the big man.

- Susanna came out of her stupor and ran quickly … straight at the cub, screaming!

- Momma stepped forward … toward Susanna!

- Mark angled and accelerated toward the bear—toward her nose?? (Some reasoning in his warrior instinct told him her nose was a sensitive spot.)

- The cub jumped backward from Susanna, heading for Momma.

- Susanna slowed slightly, but she screamed louder.

- Momma rumbled forward … to her cub.

- Mark eased up, still yelling. Susanna thought, "I have never seen my husband like this."

- Momma slowed as her cub neared her side then pivoted angrily toward Mark.

- As a warrior, he stopped to prepare for the encounter.

- Susanna also stopped. She picked up a rock, not knowing why she did it.

- Momma's cub was behind her. The she-bear was set on the big man.

- The three mature ones squared off with 30 feet between them. The cub lingered alertly at Momma's backside.

- Susanna was five feet behind Mark at an angle to his right. (She was still holding the rock.)

- Momma was mad about the 'attack' on her cub.

- Mark knew this was life or death, and all his senses intensified.

- Momma looked and circled to her right. Her cub stayed behind her.

- Mark only turned gradually. Susanna was alert standing with her husband—at ease, still holding the rock. She and Mark were one.

- And then, without a word, Susanna raised her arm and threw the rock in a slow arc. At the same instant Mark rushed toward the bear, focused on Momma's nose.

- Momma stood, wondering at the tiger-like pace of the big man! She did not notice the rock's flight.

- Susanna's stone curved through the air and landed on top of Momma's front left foot at the same instant that Mark's velocity brought him forward with a hammer-like raised fist. That large fist had been strengthened by years of wielding a hammer and sword. His hard fist struck Momma's nose like a rod of iron. The rock and the fist struck simultaneously as she bolted backward and withdrew several steps. Her nose began to bleed. She bellowed in pain.

- Mark backed up and roared three war cries that sounded like trumpet blasts.

As Momma lurched back, she checked for her cub, her nose spouting blood. She could tell this big man was not afraid. She lingered as if measuring the moment … but … her cub was fine, so Momma left with her cub. She turned as they crested the hill and gave a respectful grunt, as if to say, "I see you," and walked away.

Mark and Susanna embraced, sighed and prayed. They thanked the Lord for the deliverance from Momma. They laughed, too, as they retraced the event several times sharing the instant-by-instant impressions they had while it was happening. They were ready to leave, and as they packed up things in the wagon, Mark asked, "When did you get that rock?"

"I picked it up as we circled up together."

"Why did you throw it when you did?"

"I don't know. It just seemed the thing to do. Why did you run at her?"

"I don't know. It just seemed the thing to do."

They would laugh about that later as they told the story to their children and grandchildren again and again. They continued to laugh together, and then the Spirit of the Lord settled on them. He came in the same way He had come on their wedding night.

On their wedding day and before they had entered the marriage bed, they had knelt and prayed. They dedicated their hearts and home to the Lord. At the end of the prayer, they proclaimed, "Lord, the children that will be born as a result of our marriage, not just our first generation of children, but the grandchildren and the great-grandchildren and all the children who will be born in the generations to come; all of them, we dedicate to You and Your Kingdom. Let every child who comes through our family line, all of them resulting from our union, be dedicated to You until You return. In Jesus, Amen!"

They knew when they prayed that night at the start of their married life that they were making a divine compact. That same kind of awareness was on them now after the bears left.

So, Mark and Susanna made another commitment to each other before the Lord that day. They received this victory over the bears as a sign from the Lord and formally committed to Him and each other with these words of promise: "Any time there is a threat against us or our family, we will face it together. We will, by Your grace, great God, stand and fight as You direct us. We will come together and fight the way that You want us to fight—together. We will do it Your way. Amen!" They knew it was a holy commitment. If Mark and Susanna were anything, they were people who kept their word.

The stories inside a family can provide great strength, in the same way a foundation gives strength for a building. It was common in the culture to spend valuable time rehearsing history and life-lived via stories. The stories of pressures overcome, strength gained, the prayers that were answered and the joys celebrated are pillars for the hearts of a home. Those stories give strength to the heart of a child into the future. They provide identity and uniqueness that bolster the soul for the storms everyone must navigate. Confidence forms inside a child when they know the stories that precede their own.

James, the patriarch of the family quoted Cicero, the Greek philosopher, who said, "Not to know what happened before you were born is to remain forever a child." Family stories are a powerful tool to join the child with the family and its history. They stabilize the child's union with the family's roots and strengthen them into their tomorrows. The child's identity into the future is made stalwart.

> "Not to know what happened before you were born is to remain forever a child."

Stories can be full of power, but untold stories of darkness and shame about abuse, betrayal and pain will work in the opposite way. If they remain hidden, they will undermine the strength of a life. The evil one uses that hiddenness to wrap the mind and heart of a person with 'chains of shame.' Mark would meet several people with hidden stories—the kind that undermine a life and form chaotic chains in all they touch.

Remember, even when God came down to earth in Jesus, God told stories. They are to be told with frequency. Stories can rightly liberate the next generation from the unclean momentum of the crowded masses, who have no moorings in their soul. People with a strong story are much harder to fool.

# Chapter Four

# STORMY DIRT FROM JAPAN

"An inheritance gained quickly at the beginning
will not be blessed in the end" (Proverbs 20:21).

The Longstreet family had been blacksmiths as far back as anyone could remember, but the providential entrance of Yoshi from Japan had been a hinge event. Yoshi's arrival was a divine intrusion that turned the family into their destiny with many strong challenges.

> "A destiny found on an easy path will not be worth much."

James had often said, "A destiny found on an easy path will not be worth much."

Yoshi had brought 10 large boxes of dirt aboard the ship. He guarded those boxes with great care. One time, James' dad had left the lid off one of the boxes, and Yoshi was upset with that negligence. Transporting thousands of pounds of dirt in these 10 boxes for thousands of miles had been a herculean task. Because he knew the great capacity of this special blend of soil in making strong swords, Yoshi viewed the dirt as valuable as gold.

The family knew the dirt was from a special place in Japan with just the right mix of iron and sand for the swords. When they used that special dirt, the swords were always much stronger. Over the years, the Longstreet family had tried the other raw metals Saxons normally prepared for swords, but the native Saxon soil did not provide the strength and flexibility that came from Yoshi's dirt. Each box contained enough dirt to keep them supplied for three to four years, so initially, there was no need for more.

However, the last two boxes had lasted less than two years. This was due to the increased demand for the swords. Obviously, the supply was limited, and when the eighth box was opened, they quickly understood the need to prepare for any future service to the king and his warriors.

How they might be able to get more of this prized dirt from Japan was discussed for weeks. It would require a miracle to obtain it. James' grandfather had met Yoshi years ago on the north coast at the port in their hometown, Monkwearmout. James remembered when he first saw the boxes. They were stacked in a corner of their home forge, covered with a large heavy cloth. Yoshi's tremendous effort to bring the boxes from Japan was based on the importance of this soil for the swords. Without this special soil, the swords would not, nor could not be right. Without this soil, he had no future. The dirt was essential.

James knew the story of Yoshi from memory because storytelling was a practiced priority in the Longstreet history, and he had heard it many times. As the family gathered again to pray about what was to be done to address the unavoidable shortage, a fresh unity was formed by the urgency of the matter at hand. The prayer-peppered discussion was carried out with all the family gathered. After long considerations had been voiced by the older members of the family, a lull came over the room. Then William, the 8-year-old son of Joseph, Mark's oldest brother, spoke up with an open-hearted innocence. "Why don't we go back to the port where you met Yoshi the first time? See if someone there might know him."

All the adults knew it had been almost 20 years since Yoshi died. The older members of the family realized it was unreasonable to expect anyone there would have a connection with Yoshi or Japan. And if there was, how could they communicate the need for the dirt without exposing the secrets of the family? The idea was unreasonable. In many families that kind of comment from an 8-year-old would have been ignored at best, if not mocked and hushed as a worthless contribution.

But the honor the family walked in included the children. In the Longstreet households, everyone was respected. Mark recalled how as a child, his dad would say, "Yes, sir," whenever the children called out to him.

When he was older, Mark asked his father, "Dad, why did you call me sir when I called your name?"

"If I wanted you to learn to respect your mother and me, then I must show you that respect first."

James explained, "If I wanted you to learn to respect your mother and me, then I must show you that respect first."

Mark was impressed by the honor his father was giving to him. And so, when little William spoke, the family listened with a willing heart and did not automatically discount his words due to his youthfulness.

43

The truth was, even though the idea was strange to their minds, they had to admit an unusual peace settled into their hearts the moment William voiced it. Mark spoke what several of them sensed. "That may be the very thing we are to do." James nodded in agreement along with others.

Elizabeth looked at James and Mark as she said, "Let's pray and determine when you two can make that journey."

So, they prayed, gave thanks, and planned the best time to go to the northern shore to see if there would be a way to connect with someone who might know how to get more of the dirt from Japan. They expected to leave before the spring thaw. They wanted to be back for the planting season. Although they were blacksmiths, they still had to plow, plant, tend and harvest crops each year. The days were full.

Mark was only 16 years old when the trip was planned, yet his form and strength were astonishing. Grown men often guessed he was 8-10 years older. He simply carried himself as a mature man. This internal stability emanated from him as a calming yet vigorous capacity. Few were willing to test their own strength against his, and those who did, were always disappointed with the outcome.

Regarding his own strength, Mark had often wondered why Delilah, in the Bible story had to ask Samson where he got his strength from. Apparently, Samson did not appear physically strong. His physical form was not the source of his power, else why would she have asked the question? Mark reasoned it was indeed the Lord's Spirit coming on Samson that empowered him.

Bible stories and the words of Jesus formed the primary grid through which their family had framed their perspective about all of life. This had proved wise and beneficial every time.

James and Mark left in early March on the three-day journey northward. There were two friends along the route, whose houses were spaced in such a way that they could spend the evenings in those homes without being an inconvenience. The trip was cold but uneventful. They arrived late on the third day.

Normally, they would have stayed at the monastery, but it was overwhelmed with travelers from the south who had come for a Church Festival. So, they took the last room in a musty ramshackle inn. One wall was sliced with frequent cracks through which the outside entered easily. Sometimes the walls 'whistled' as the wind blew. The floorboards were similarly rippled and sloping. But they were glad for a place to rest. After they had put their things in the small space, some rain began to fall easily enough, but it rapidly increased in strength and began to fall forcefully with a persistent staccato thrum.

The rain was drenching and brought cold winds that lasted two days without letting up. The dirt lane outside was transformed. It became furrowed with flowing streams of mud. It was far too hazardous to go out. They had food and drink at the inn, so they remained in the damp building with seven men. These seven had also found refuge at the inn from the unforeseen deluge. The smoke from the fire filtered out most of the dank rot emitted by the old, cold structure.

The strong wind and rain coerced a fresh fellowship upon these nine current strangers. James and Mark knew the Bible gave directions about how to serve and care for strangers, but it also taught the wisdom of guarding your mouth and ears while with those you did not know. The stormy circumstances composed these men into a willing, yet wary informal circle. They came together with both of those characteristics. They did not yet know that it was a providentially arranged assembly, at least for James and Mark it was. The benefits of this 'happenstance' would grow into the future for the Longstreet men.

The seven other men were: a young monk, who was crossing the North Sea to begin his newly commissioned assignment from the monastery in Monkwearmout. He had given up his room at the monastery for the festival-people. Another, about James' age, carried himself with a special dignity, despite walking with a slight limp. Then two brothers returning from business in northern Europe, had stopped at the inn due to fatigue. They only had one more day to reach home. They were younger and spoke some, but not too often since they understood the wisdom of yielding to the older men in the circle.

A tragedy had forced a journey on a father and son who were headed south for work opportunities. They were enduring the recent death of the wife and mother from lung problems. They were starting over. The aroma of unresolved grief was present in them. The last, the seventh was older, with deep blue eyes, and his head was crowned with more gray hair than brown. He rarely spoke, but he listened intently to all that was shared. Mark recognized this old man was catching every nuance of the words expressed and the hearts that spoke them. Mark wondered about him from the outset. Several times over the next two days, Mark sensed a strong holiness in him. There was a sacred fear on him. This seventh man was different.

The storm was not letting up soon. Since that was the case, stories began to pass between them. Slowly at first and not too profoundly, they began to share. But as the hours persisted, the courage to make friendships developed. The wealth gained by open-hearted conversation began to take root. The common walls between hearts fell.

The dignified man with the limp, who acted as if he was a noble, was the captain of a trading vessel. His family had served on sailing ships for generations. His name was Charles. The captain had some of the most exciting stories.

They spoke for hours with the driving rain as a backdrop. There were tears a few times, prompted by somber or tender tales. Number seven spoke of a painful season years ago when he lost his wife. The man and his son cried freely, as the old man's story cut open their recent grief. With no shame from the circle, all allowed these old and new griefs to be silently recognized. Others shared near-death experiences along with the scars to verify their account.

The stories broached all manner of topics, soon venturing into much loud laughing, which tends to occur when an all-male assembly has convened. The monk shared stories that had all of them laughing raucously. He spoke of one memory about the leader of the monastery, who though he was a large-framed man, walked as a man of honor and dignity. The leader had become stuck crossing a fence when they were gathering wild berries one day. As the monk recalled the event, it was obvious he was going back to that moment in his mind. He told us the story and the comical appearance of the senior leader stuck in the fence was forming in his mind's eye.

The other monks began to slowly grin, seeing the leader stuck. As he told us the story, the monk paused for a few seconds as the image re-formed inside his mind's eye. A large smile formed on his face. He was remembering. The past became the present. The former, funny moment was now the present. In his mind, he had set the monk's normal dignity and formality next to the current image of his large frame stuck in the fence. He exploded in a laughter that caused everyone else to laugh. We were laughing more because of how hard the monk was laughing than about the story.

James and Mark spoke of their family. James casually mentioned his blacksmith trade, but he said nothing of the sword that bore the family name. The stories rambled on and crossed into the many lands of 'social geography' as the hours of those two days and nights played out.

The unplanned rest became a wonderful time of friendship. Then late in the evening of the second day, as the rain was slowing down, the conversation turned to unusual people they had met. The captain of the ship spoke offhandedly of an odd Japanese man his grandfather had known. James and Mark found themselves standing at attention on the inside, yet they gave no external expression. *Could this man have known Yoshi?*

An hour later, all nine men were correctly expecting this would be the last night in the inn. The rain was easing its harsh washings, and the morning should provide the opportunity to go their separate ways. When the circle of men began to lose its formal setting and disintegrate, James approached the captain, "Did you say your grandfather knew a man from Japan?"

"Yes, I did. His name was … uh … uh …

"Yoshi?"

"Yes, I think that was it."

James and Mark smiled and asked if they might have a few more minutes of his time.

"Of course," he said. "We aren't leaving until the day after tomorrow. The rain has slowed the loading of our ship. I am in no hurry."

After hearing the stories of these seven men, James and Mark had sensed a deeper comradery with Captain Charles than with the others. Charles began to tell the story. The longer he spoke, the more they smiled. They were in awe of the Lord and His supernatural directing of their steps. He had used the rain to arrange this chance meeting with Charles. It was wonderful. Captain Charles was the grandson of the man with whom Yoshi had booked his passage from the continent across the North Sea to the Saxon port. In addition, Charles knew many more details of Yoshi's story than the Longstreet family had learned.

Yoshi had been a blacksmith for nobility in Japan. He was accused by one of the royal families of defrauding the honor of a young lady and she was the daughter of a prince. The girl denied any dishonor by Yoshi, but the prince stubbornly refused to hear it. Yoshi steadfastly proclaimed he had done no wrong. But the man who accused him was unrelenting, refusing to stop until the lady's honor was appropriately vindicated by Yoshi's death.

49

Yoshi had a two-week head start in leaving. A sudden invasion by a band of rebels forced the prince to defend the city. Yoshi secretly and tearfully said good-bye to the young princess and used the delay for the prince to cover his escape. His items to take included 10 boxes of the sword-dirt. It was that valuable to him. He took his wagon on a route used mainly by farmers; by avoiding the normal travel lanes, he hoped to confuse his pursuer. He drove a meandering course to the western coast of Japan and planned to board a ship for China. From there he would go farther, but where and how far he did not yet know. He was on the run.

Yoshi made it to China, and after vaguely discussing his wishes with some traders, he chose to travel west on the Silk Road. This was the name of an established network of travel routes that connected the East and West. It included both sea and land pathways. Due to roving bands of bandits, either way was dangerous. Robbers are often lazy men, who want riches without working. The Silk Road stretched all the way into the Mediterranean Sea, and Yoshi decided to go the sea route and travel as far as possible.

Yoshi needed to start a new life, and yet, the grief of the loss of his love was a burden he carried that was as heavy as the boxes. The Silk Road had been used for hundreds of years, and was often crowded with many kinds of travelers, threats and opportunities. The land passage would have taken take him north of the Himalayas, and the boxes of dirt would make land travel much more difficult. The sea route led ultimately to the west coast of Italy. His journey across Asia and Europe would take over 20 months. There were weeks he had to stop and work to make money. The days spent working were rarely restful, since he was on constant watch for the persistent prince who was chasing him—at least he thought the prince would be pursuing him.

Those months were a furnace of pressure and threat and always looking over his shoulder for his 'imagined' pursuer bent on revenge. Yoshi traveled in three different ships, through two harsh storms, endured a nighttime attack by a large sea creature and two attacks by pirates. But even the pirates saw no value in his boxes of dirt. They were a burden too heavy to steal. For Yoshi, they were a benefit too valuable to forsake.

With each transition of the ships used came the exhausting task of unloading and then reloading the boxes. Yoshi carried his seemingly valueless dirt quietly and without complaint. He knew the prospect of great wealth resident in the sand and iron mix. He felt strongly about the secrets the dirt provided, and he knew the dirt would unlock a powerful destiny for someone, someone significant. For Yoshi, it became a sacred trek. Yoshi began to realize that the value of the dirt was not for him, but for someone else to gain.

As Yoshi journeyed, he was more and more persuaded that a kind of divine grip was on his life. He became convinced his trek was an effort to discover who this dirt was for. The pressures of the journey and this dawning recognition in his heart were changing him. He became a more peaceful man, and this forced trek caused him to wonder about the One Who made all things as he carried the dirt in this exodus from Japan. The poison of resentment formed by the accusation against him began to leak away. He frequently spent the evenings alone on the decks of the boats gazing at the stars. He began to consider the great One Who knew all things and held all things together.

After making it to the Sea east of Italy's boot, he chose to continue north into the Frankish empire. He was still not at ease from his pursuer. Yoshi worked for two months with a local blacksmith and purchased a wagon and six horses to carry the boxes. He used that wagon to transport the boxes to the northern coasts of Europe. Finally, he arrived in northwestern Europe. He had come to a Danish port on the North Sea, the same one where Yoshi met Charles' grandfather. Yoshi saw the captain with his ship. He approached and requested passage for his final sea crossing. He was hoping it would conclude his effort to get away from the prince. He believed he had gone far enough.

Yoshi, who up until his encounter with Charles' grandfather had shared his adventure with no one, found himself telling the details of his heart. The prince-pursuer and the accusation against him had combined to squelch any previous release of the story. But the story had come out of him unintentionally when he understood there was no threat of judgment against him in Saxon lands. The pressure of his aloneness forced the story out. It came in broken sentences of Saxon and Frankish phrases, all which he had picked up during his travels.

The heretofore internal and unspoken ponderings of his story seemed strange when he heard them voiced for the first time by his own mouth. When they were only known in the secret places of his internal wonderings, they were more believable.

But in the light of spoken disclosure, they made his story appear childish and silly. But Charles' grandfather cradled the story and the dream for the dirt with kind ears and a receptive heart. He said, "It sounds like the Lord has His hand on you, Sir."

Yoshi would ultimately hear from godly men how the Lord was overseeing his odyssey for His purposes. He was told the amazing account of Joseph, who was betrayed by his brothers, sold into slavery, and falsely accused by Potiphar's wife and wrongfully put into prison. This tale touched Yoshi profoundly. The Lord had used that hammer of injustice to place iron into Joseph's soul. (Psalm 105:18).

Yoshi told the story in detail to Charles' grandfather. He concluded, "I like Josep, I not do rong I cused of." But he also sensed the prince would never give up. He had traveled many wandering vectors to break any grip the prince had on his footsteps.

Charles' grandfather later said, "When that Japanese man was first talking to me, I knew I would say "yes" to whatever he asked me. I do not know why I felt that, but I simply knew I would say "yes." There was something about this man from Japan that made me want to help him. I had my men unload his wagon laden with the boxes of dirt and put them on board. My ship was light because I had unloaded my cargo. The boxes provided some ballast for the trip back to Saxon ground. So, he came with us."

After arriving on Saxony's northern shores, Yoshi stayed with Charles' family for a month. When James' grandfather had met Yoshi in town, he discovered Yoshi was also a blacksmith.

Yoshi and James' grandfather found an immediate kinship.

James then told Charles, "My grandfather reported the same to us as your grandfather did to you. He said, "There was simply something about the man that made me want to help him. So, he came to live with us too.""

Captain Charles, James and Mark stayed up late into the night reviewing the story. The Longstreet men had an awareness they could trust Charles with some of the details of their secret. They spoke of the special blend of iron and sand in this dirt and how, for some reason, the dirt was essential to making their swords so strong. Then they said, "We need more of the dirt. It will be gone in the next two years. Do you know anyone who might be able to help us get this kind of dirt from Japan?"

Charles was amazed at the bold request from these new friends, but he was not troubled by the question. However, he was speechless. Then Charles explained that just two weeks earlier, he encountered a man from Japan at the Lundabyarg port. It was on the southern end of the Danish peninsula where his grandfather met Yoshi. The man had been working for several years as a trader from Asia.

"Two weeks ago, I told that man from Japan I would come back this month to discuss possible items he might supply in trade with us and what we could exchange with him," said Ch arles.

Now, James and Mark were stunned. *"Was it going to be that simple?"* After a few moments, more questions flew …
"Could this man know how to get this dirt? Would he be willing to search? Was this even real? Who gets dirt from another

54

nation?" They rattled off numerous ideas and still wondered if this was possible.

They concluded God had ordered their steps to be here at this time, later remarking, "Well, we did ask the Lord to direct us. We should have expected Him to do something wonderful."

"I will be going back to meet him next week," Charles replied. "He and I will be here three weeks from today. He wants to see our port to understand its depth and details. If you want to come back then, we can all speak with him."

James and Mark agreed to return in a few weeks. They went to bed in the early hours of the coming dawn in amazement. Just a few hours of sleep passed, and both were awake and ready to go home. The storm delay had created a readiness to get back to their family. Morning came with a welcoming warm, clear sky. The men, who had shared their stories during the storm, were all saying farewell to one another. Only the seventh man, the old man with the bright eyes was absent. James and Mark had wondered aloud, if maybe he had been an angel assisting them in their purpose. They thanked God for him, whether he was an angel or not.

In a remarkable display of surprises, James returned a few weeks later with another son and met the man from Japan. And again, unusual benefits occurred. The man was indeed familiar with the region where the dirt could be found and believed he could provide it to them. After two hours of deliberation, an agreement on price was reached and the particulars of the transaction were settled. James paid the man half the price requested by the Japanese trader with Captain Charles as a witness. The Japanese man gave them a family jewel as a promise to return next year with the dirt.

When James came home from the second trip, the family rejoiced at his report, and the details of that story were added to the story of the three days in the rain. These two narratives were added to the family's treasure-book of stories.

The major concern, besides the logistical burdens for the trip, was whether this man would keep his promise to come back in a year. They had to trust his integrity. The agreement had been made for 15 boxes.

Thirteen months later, Captain Charles messaged the family via a courier that he was ready to cross the North Sea to go to the Danish port expecting to meet the man.

The next morning, James and Mark rode the family wagon to Monkwearmout. They would travel with Captain Charles across the North Sea and meet the man in Lundabyarg. After boarding, they crossed an unusually calm sea. The man from Japan had arrived 10 days earlier with 14 boxes of 'sword-dirt.' One box had been lost crossing a river in Frankish territory. James gladly paid the remaining price and returned the man's family jewel. The boxes were loaded on board; they positioned them down the center line of the hull in the cargo hold. The two Longstreet men, Captain Charles and the Japanese man ate dinner together, which led to another night of storytelling.

The sun broke through the morning with hope and promise. The faithful man from Japan bid them farewell with some sort of Japanese blessing and was thanked for his faithful service. A favorable breeze was blowing bright, white clouds as they embarked for the crossing of the North Sea. It was expected the promising breeze would gently assist them on their journey. But the breeze did not keep its' promise. The sea and the sky changed severely after they entered open water.

Four things rose violently in a matter of minutes: much colder air, black clouds, harsh winds and awkwardly uneven brutish waves. The wind was in charge, and Charles' face belied the uncertainty of the moment. They were driven northeasterly, off course. They could do nothing but pray as the crew scurried around the deck without words. James and Mark were not seamen. They were familiar with ground that did not move and provided sure footing. This instability unnerved them. The entire world seemed made of jelly.

After all the blessings, was their anticipation of fulfillment to be shattered in the sea? The waves were 25 feet tall, and the ship was reeling front to back, then side to side—it was a wonder they did not capsize.

Mark and James were praying and considering the storms in the Bible: Jonah's disobedient flight away from Nineveh; Paul's two-week-long storm on the way to Rome; and the reference in Psalm 107:23-28, which says of those in storms,

> "Those that do business on great waters …
> their soul melts because of trouble, they reel to
> and fro, and are at their wits' end. Then they cry
> out to the Lord in their trouble and He brings
> them out of their distresses."

The Longstreet men cried out to the Lord in their trouble.

They found their confidence to go through the storm bolstered by that divine promise. The storm lasted all night and drove them many leagues away from their intended heading. But by morning, Captain Charles said they could turn and make for home. Later that day, Charles explained the thousands of pounds of dirt they had in the hold of the ship was the reason why they had not capsized. The dirt provided the ballast needed to keep the ship upright. The Lord was working out all the details.

James and Mark were quick to personally and specifically give thanks to the Lord for the deliverance. They did not attribute it to luck or good fortune. They knew all too well that being grateful is a key element of healthy living.

> They knew all too well that being grateful is a key element of healthy living.

They arrived a day later at the northern port of Monkwearmout. Since they were a day and a half behind their planned arrival, the cargo that was to be loaded to go on the return trip was waiting on the dock, guarded by dock workers. Both Saxon men assisted harbor workers in carrying their boxes off and placing them in a wagon. James and Mark were exhausted from the stormy, sleepless night and the long day. So, they decided to overnight at the monastery where Saint Bede had studied. There was no festival in town this time.

They fell into the beds graciously provided by the monks. It was after midnight and sleep gripped their bodies strongly. They wakened later than usual, and after breakfast, walked around the back of the building to discover that one of the 14 boxes of dirt had been taken from the wagon. The wagon had been placed by itself behind the back wall, the only place with room in the small, but expertly manicured grounds. Wheel tracks from a small wagon could be seen in the dirt along with the footprints of four or five men. (Mark found out years later one of the ship hands had overheard a conversation with the Captain and surmised the dirt was valuable in making swords, but that was all he knew. That ship hand had a friend who was not upright in conduct. The two of them had hatched the scheme to take the box in the early morning hours.)

The theft was a sour note in the melody of this song. But, the 13 boxes of dirt were reckoned better than nothing, and the loss was not going to ruin the grace the Lord had provided. They continued to be full of thanks to Him for a safe return.

The Longstreet family was full of stories, and these journeys would be gathered with the litany of the family's other memories. This was the first of the sea stories in the family history. But it would not be the last.

Yoshi's story would have a footnote. That 'note' came less than two years later when the last of Yoshi's 10 boxes were opened. A cryptic note was found inside the box on top of the dirt. It was written awkwardly using the few words he had learned to write.

"Yoshi not spek light to longstret fater … Yoshi lov lady … Yoshi wit lady … king's son right to cum for Yoshi … many days. Yoshi heart full wit dark words … Yoshi spek now in light to gret God … Yoshi spek to Him of dark hiding … ask gret God to wash Yoshi

of dark … ask Him to wash with blud of Son … Yoshi
clean wit Him … Yoshi ned be light wit you … please
furgiv … tank longstrets for lov."

# Chapter Five

# GLAD DAYS

Proverbs 17:22 states, "A merry heart does good, like a medicine."

"I will open my mouth in a parable; I will utter dark sayings of old, which we have heard and known, and our fathers have told us. We will not hide them from their children. We will tell the generation to come the praises of the Lord, and His strength and His wonderful works that He has done. For He established a testimony in Jacob, and appointed a law in Israel which He commanded our fathers, that they should make them known to their children; that the generation to come might know them, the children who would be born, that they may arise and declare them to their children, that they may set their hope in God, and not forget the works of God, but keep His commandments." Psalm 78:2-7.

The abundance of good things, which come from the stability generated by right living, is hard to explain to anyone

> He commanded our fathers, that they should make them known to their children; that the generation to come might know them, the children who would be born, that they may arise and declare them to their children, that they may set their hope in God, and not forget the works of God, but keep His commandments."

who has not received or invested their family's heart into such worthwhile priorities. Many people must work at having fun. They must plan the time to party or go to the festival or the sports event, so they can have a good time.

The truth is that many people do not have gladness as a part of their everyday living. They struggle to be joyful without some sort of prop as an external stimulus to be happy. The routines of life seem meaningless, and good times must be orchestrated or purposely positioned. They need to be artificially propelled into glad places by some chemical blend to make them feel better, at least for a few hours. They go to the tavern after a day's work because they do not want to face the family drudgery, or the weekend mead becomes a sedative to numb the voice of the void inside. For some, work and alcohol are the primary ingredients of their existence.

The Longstreet family never experienced that degree of boredom, nor did they search for artificial supports to find joy. Their gladness came organically out of life shared, and the laughter was inherent due to the love, unity and work they enjoyed together. In any family, each person is unique, and the Longstreet clan celebrated each one's particular way.

All the children were physically capable and distinctive. Aaron was the most like his father mentally and carried deep insights about life. Christopher blended a kind heart, hard work and a warrior's will, with the strength of an ox. Zechariah was the prophet of the group and merged strength of body with spiritual precision. Jennifer was the spark of life in every circumstance and moved as her mother did, with insight and courage. She was willing to make bold moves as she trusted the Lord. Michaela was the most unusual and seemed more heavenly minded from the beginning of her life. She spoke less often than the other children, but when she did, something of a deeply divine viewpoint was working in her. She seemed angelic from birth. Everything about her made you consider heavenly ideas. She was different. She was more heavenly than earthly. She was more present there than here.

Embroidered through their differences was the kind of quick wit that could generate waves of laughter. And then, more serious topics would arise, which they could engage with even greater ease since the family was founded on a strong base of love and truth. Because the adults studied, prayed and reasoned through life based on the Scriptures, the children viewed life from a strong and clear ethical base. Their minds were not dulled or slow. The ability to think and reason clearly from a spiritual strength is a gift from God. This settles one into an internal clarity undefiled by the world's priorities.

> The ability to think and reason clearly from a spiritual strength is a gift from God. This settles one into an internal clarity undefiled by the world's priorities.

God intended humans to steward the earth. The first thing He spoke over Adam and Eve was to rule the earth. (Genesis 1:25, 26). The view the Longstreet family had of the world was framed from that biblical clarity. Therefore, it was no accident the family was stable and unfettered by the culture's commonly held dreads or fears. They never saw the Lord as oppressive or mean. A monk from the monastery who visited the church had often said, "We consistently misunderstand how willing the Lord is to share His power with us. We must not use His power for our own purposes, but as we cooperate with His motives, we can gain a wonder-filled life."

> "We consistently misunderstand how willing the Lord is to share His power with us."

They received, planned, and implemented the Word of God with purpose and consistency. Sure, the children had typical fits and spats that children the world over participate in, but the healthy roots of the Longstreet line supplied the family with a peace that enabled them to enjoy life more than most. Joy is hard to receive or express if your 'inside-life' is unstable.

One evening, during an unforgettable supper that continued for nearly three hours, an especially memorable and complex exchange took place. Susanna and Mark were laughing as much as the children. The stories kept coming. First, there was the time Aaron fell through a bedroom wall with his backside breaking a wooden support. Then Jennifer recalled the time she spent an hour washing a piglet, which immediately after the bath, scampered off to 'clean' itself in the mud. Next came the story of how Mark was being silly with the two oldest boys when he fell into a water trough, and no one could forget the time Christopher, though smaller than Mark and when he was only 14 years old, had come up behind his dad while the family played in a river. He quickly wrapped his arms around Mark's waist, and then began to lift him over his head and backflipped

Mark into the river behind him.

Mark was astonished, and so was everyone who saw it. Mark testified later that no one had ever flipped his body like that. Zechariah's addition to the family's funny events included the time he threw a wooden ball against a wall, and it came back and hit him on the lip. Each story became funnier than the one before. Hard laughter over a long period of time becomes wonderfully fatiguing.

Some of the younger children did not remember a story or simply had not been born when it happened, which gave the older ones a chance to fill in the details and rehearse it. The second telling would create more laughter than the first time through.

When the entire group was smiling hard and all were tired from laughing so long, the family helped Susanna clean up from dinner and prepared for bed. Lastly, they gathered for the evening prayer time. They had been going through the Gospel of Mark by memory from the monk's lessons at the church and were talking about the time Jesus drove at least 2,000 demons from the Gadarene demoniac. This account had always intrigued Mark, and he told it with a genuine enthusiasm.

You cannot generate this kind of authentic interest in the Word of God unless you are a true follower of Jesus. Mark came to the point in the story where the monk had increased the volume of his voice, saying, "Jesus directed the demons to be dismissed into the pigs. The demons entered the pigs, and then the pigs went into the sea and were choked in the sea!"

The family never quite understood why, but Mark stopped

in the middle of the story and waited just a moment as he was considering something. Then with a strange facial expression, he posed two questions: "Can you imagine what devils in pigs look like? Who has ever heard of 'deviled ham?'"

Something about his facial expression, the strange tone of his voice and his unusual term 'deviled ham,' combined with three prior hours of laughing caused the house to erupt with hilarious laughter for another 15 minutes. Deviled ham became the family word for weirdly appearing circumstances. The family spoke of that night many times in the future and would laugh all over again.

The strength of the Word of God and its joys and revelation of Jesus had first been deposited in Mark's great-grandfather. There was a monastery in Monkwearmout, which was the first base of training for Bede (later known as the Venerable Bede). Bede became one of the great theologians and historians of his day, and his extending influence included blessing the Longstreet family for several years.

Bede was a busy writer and a strong communicator of the truth. He was held in high regard because he held the Lord and His Word in high regard. He coined the term *Anno Domini* (A.D.) in his writings, because Jesus began a new epoch for the whole world and had come not only to save us, but to change the world and its times. So, it was utterly reasonable to Bede to establish the order of the years based on what we could become after Jesus came.

Bede was a young man, but he spent many hours with Mark's great-grandfather and grandfather discussing the Lord and His Word. The whole area had been impacted by Bede's ministry and St. Patrick's miraculous works and ways continued to impact the history of the land, though he had died almost 300 years earlier. With that kind of rich deposit into the family, it was not strange to see those truths continue in the family.

Joy and laughter were the norm for the Longstreet home. People often commented on the peace they felt in the house, even with five children. One lady, who had been mistreated as a child, stayed with James and Elizabeth for a week. She was disconnected from herself because of horrific abuses she had endured. After two days in the family, she was quite anxious, fearing the house was too peaceful. She wondered out loud, "When does the screaming start?"

The family told her, "We don't do that here ... ever." That week with the Longstreet family was a healing balm for her life. Many more glad days than sad days ruled their life. They lived within a supernatural blessing.

# Chapter Six

# ROUND ONE–THE SECOND MEETING WITH ERIK

Susanna had never told Mark about the time she hit Erik, had broken his tooth, and made him deaf in one ear. And Mark had never told her about the guy who had run into him when he first moved to the castle. The topic never came up. For Mark, it was an odd, meaningless encounter, and for Susanna the rude trespass by Erik was, as far as she was concerned, something to forget. But that rude trespass and the odd run-in were merging, and the results of that convergence would deeply hurt them both.

Sons of Baal create chaos. They enjoy havoc. They always make things worse. Fools such as them never add benefits to a situation.

Mark and Susanna were at the market to see what fresh vegetables might be available. The beans should be ready now, and Susanna had been told by her good friend, NanLee Smithson, that the cabbages had come in. Mark always enjoyed showing off Susanna. They had been married for almost three years and were spending the morning in the plaza. She was delightful to be with. Much like Mark's mom, Elizabeth, who carried herself with a stately decorum that attracted honor,

Susanna also moved in a feminine dignity without the slightest bit of arrogance or smugness.

The town plaza had been turned into a marketplace offering many differing fares. Wagons and tables were ordered into an angled-oval arc, connecting just outside the main gate. Mark noticed a fellow member of the guard and walked away from Susanna to speak with him. She went on to investigate the quality of some apples on the back of a wagon.

She had looked up from the cart and recognized Erik's form about 50 feet away. Her heart skipped a beat, but she was glad his back was turned. Looking immediately for Mark, she found his eyes and motioned for him. But turning her gaze back in the direction of Erik, she stiffened inside. Erik was looking directly at her and had begun walking toward her. Susanna whirled and walked/ran for her husband.

As Mark moved toward her, he noticed Erik looking at Susanna and the concern in her steps. He also had a disconcerting sense of Erik's focus on Susanna. Mark was always alert, but this guy did not look right. Mark accelerated his pace, closing the gap between him and Susanna. The doesn't-look-right-guy focused his gaze on her. He was not aware of Mark. Mark was about to redirect Erik's attention.

Almost simultaneously, Susanna stepped into Mark's brief embrace and Erik finally saw the big man. Erik's advance was halted by Mark's massive frame and then his straightforward greeting. "Sir, what business do you have with my wife?" Mark interjected his inquiry with firmness.

Erik was taken back by Mark's use of the word 'wife.' He

looked up at Mark's broad ox-like strong body, and then he vividly remembered the run-in against the wall-man more than two years before. He recalled fully and angrily. *"Yes, that had been the same day she slapped me toothless and deaf."* Erik reddened as it dawned on him that Susanna and Mark were married. "Well, your wife," he retorted with evident bitterness, "broke my tooth and slapped me deaf in this ear," motioning to the left side of his head. He never took his fiery eyes away from Susanna.

Mark stepped in front of Erik and answered gently, "Sir, if my wife slapped you, I am sure you deserved it. For someone of your stubbornness to be dealt with at all by a woman of her excellence should be considered a great honor."

Mark's casual tone coupled with the rebuke created a problem for Erik. Everyone else became intimidated or fearful when Erik was angry. But this guy, this big man was calm. Erik was unnerved. Mark's peacefulness rendered Erik unpeaceful. Erik spit the words out through clinched teeth, "Your wife? It's not right! She was supposed to be with me!"

Mark continued as if he was in an everyday conversation, "Based on what agreement, Sir? Did you speak with her parents? Did she ever agree to be with you for even one social event? Did she ever give any indication of interest in you? I think you assumed far too much, Sir. It is best for you to move on, now."

Erik was upset with himself because he was losing control inside, and all the answers to Mark's questions were a loud and painful interior *"No."* But it was that last word Mark had spoken—the *now*, which raised Erik's ire. That word had a slight rise in pitch and was obviously spoken as an order. Erik hated orders. That *now* ignited the flame of pain in him. He didn't care how big this guy was.

With a quickness and agility most would have been startled by, the kind of speedy motion gained only through multiplied hours of skilled training, Erik filled his right hand with a knife out of nowhere. It sported a sharp and deadly 12-inch blade. The hand holding it was all too steady and obviously well-acquainted with how to use it.

Mark knew this angry man was serious, and once again, he was without his sword. He had to accept for the second time, the same internal correction as occurred with the bears. He knew now that he must never be without his sword again. But for the moment, he needed to reckon with a knife held by an enraged and skilled man.

Erik had backed up a half step to give himself more room to maneuver. The descending sun glinted off the razor-sharp edge of the weapon. Mark moved Susanna further back behind him without ever taking his eye off the knife or the eyes of the man holding it. With a gentle but firm pivoting of Susanna behind him, the air silenced, and the marketplace became aware of this encounter. The people backed up to give them room, yet no one left. Most of them knew Erik, and all knew Mark.

The crowd was thinking, *"This interchange could be very interesting."*

Mark was a man of honor, and he gave that same honor to all who knew him; yet it is not easy to give honor to someone who is not honorable. This was the kind of intersection in life where the truly righteous ones are at a disadvantage, at least as far as the world thinks. But the promise of God states, "The eyes of the Lord run to and fro throughout the whole earth to strongly support those whose hearts are completely His."

Mark's primary concern was not first to protect his wife or to overcome this man. His priority was to please the Lord while he did those two things. *And by God's grace, he would do those two things.* Mark was calm because he still remembered in painfully vivid, slow-motion images, the damage his anger had done and the picture of Wayne's body spinning off the top of that rock years ago.

Remaining righteous in our actions is not easy when strong carnal desires rise to release all our anger, especially against a son of Baal who deserves it. But to deal with Erik in the same kind of anger he was displaying would be agreeing with the enemy's scheme. Mark would work with this man in a righteous way.

The next second was filled with such speed that few discerned it as it happened. After the fact, people realized what he had done and how quickly he had done it. Mark did not move his feet. He had never backed up. Mark's penetrating eyes were staring deeply into Erik's, but Erik was completely stunned at how quickly Mark did what he did.

Some people knew that Mark had been rehearsing with a sword all his life. As a child he had played with fake swords and small hammers in the same way his father worked with real ones. But Mark played with the hammer and sword using both his right and left hands, because early on, he recognized his right side was growing stronger than the left. Mark wisely understood the need for both hands and arms to be equal in strength and coordination, so he began to alternate hands when working with the hammer and practicing with the sword. He had continued alternating hands every day. He was as good and strong with his left as he was with the right.

But Erik also knew he was good with his knife. He had forged it himself, and the scars on the bodies of several men proved how good he was at using it. His most proud boast was that he had no scars on his own body, not one! He had never been cut by anyone during the scores of knife-fights he had started. Now, he was fully alert, slightly crouched, ready to strike and mentally preparing for his first feint. He would get the big guy off balance and then scar another man no matter how big he was. As far as Erik was concerned, this big man had to be humiliated. This big man had too much pride. Erik always thought any confident man was too proud.

Instead, Erik was not ready for Mark's speed. He never saw it coming. The movement Mark employed, and the suddenness of it was unimaginable. Erik could not accept a man that big could move that fast. In one action, two things occurred. Mark's left hand flew to the outside of the knife in Erik's right. In the same moment, Mark's right hand moved to the inside wrist of Erik's right. At the same time: Erik's wrist was broken with an ugly juicy snap. As he winced and bent over, he lost his grip on the knife's handle. Mark's left hand grabbed the loosened blade and suddenly, Mark had the knife. Then immediately, without thinking, Mark swiped the blade with a reflex, an explosion of skill, and sliced a two-inch cut across Erik's chin. The fight was over.

Erik grimaced from his broken wrist, the humiliation of the people clapping and more than anything, the bleeding cut on his chin. He was seething because no one had cut him before. Mark had marked him. He had never been so angry.

Mark spoke calmly, "Sir."

Erik interrupted with staunch exclamations uttered with forceful maliciousness.

"Stop calling me 'Sir!' The name is Erik! You will never forget me! We will meet again, and neither you nor your wife will be happy at the end of that! That is a promise I will keep!"

The *keep* was barked out with a strong emphasis.

Once again, Mark replied with his normal peaceful composure, "Erik, it is best for you to move on. I will hold your well-made knife—at least until you can show the kind of proper self-control and honor to deserve carrying such an excellent weapon. But if we do meet again, you had better come with a heart willing to apologize to my wife. She is worthy of that and God will bless you for the humility."

Erik was grabbing for the final word. He growled like a brute beast. "By God, we will meet again, and you will never forget it!"

He walked away, bleeding from his chin and holding his wrist, making an internal vow, "*I will kill that man, even if he did say my knife was 'well-made.'* Mark's compliment of the knife notwithstanding, the seeds for his plan of revenge were generated before he was 100 yards away.

While Erik sulked off, Susanna slipped firmly into Mark's large strong embrace. They stood for a moment in silence. Then he spoke as if questioning what someone thought of the weather, "Do you have something to tell me?" She smiled and thanked him for protecting her from Erik. Then she recounted the times Erik had tried to woo her with flowers and a necklace, and his embrace and the attempted kiss.

"You were right—I never gave him any indication of interest." She also explained how she had slapped him. "That's what he was saying about his tooth and hearing loss."

Mark smiled, "I knew I married a courageous lady."

Some of the crowd gathered around and thanked Mark for dealing with Erik so well.

"He is such a mean man," said one.

"Erik always causes trouble," added another man amid the words from those bringing judgment.

Then one lady said, "Erik hurt my brother so badly, he was unable to walk for two months."

Mrs. Dawson, an older lady, expressed a completely different perspective, "I think he is a lonely, pain-filled man," she said with sadness. "My father knew Erik's dad and told us he was mean as a viper, but I think we ought to pray for him."

A seasoned elder spoke up, "The good thing is he lives far away, and he only comes to the castle twice a year for supplies. The bad news is that he has some young men who follow him, and he trains them. They have his same meanness in them. They are suspected of stealing equipment and weapons. Some even think his band is responsible for two deaths we cannot solve."

Many others spoke badly about him, but they were all grateful for Mark's skill in stopping Erik.

One person chimed in with this praise of Mark, "The King will be proud of you!" The crowd roared and clapped in agreement. The words secretly sank into a sweet place of Mark's heart. He would treasure those words … treasure them too much.

After the crowd drifted away, the elder approached Mark with a steady gaze, he spoke quietly and intently, "Erik is an evil man. He has been that way from early in his life. A devastating event broke whatever tenderness his heart may have held. His mom died in a fire when he was 8 years old. The strength of that grief twisted him like a rope. He will keep his promise. He will come back, and that blaze of rage in him will do nothing except get hotter. Next time, you won't surprise him. And just so you know, Erik made that knife for himself. He prizes it."

As he lay in bed that night with Susanna asleep by his side, Mark considered the fight with Erik. He replayed each action in the eyes and ears of his mind. He registered the focus and speed of Erik's moves and knew the next time he would not be able to catch him off guard. The elder had said Erik's mom had died in a fire when he was 8 years old—the same age Mark had been when he ruined Wayne's ability to run. The old pain came back. He prayed.

Later, he looked at the knife he had taken from Erik. The knife was well-made and forged with an unusual strength. Erik had made the knife for his own hand. *"I stole it from him."* Mark wondered then, *"So, I will fight with a blacksmith."* The knife's edge was as sharp as Mark's sword. Only the grace of God had prevented him from cutting his hand as he snatched it. But the memory most embossed in his recollections was the acute awareness of a demonic presence speaking when Erik vowed Mark would never forget him, and neither he nor Susanna would like the end when they met again.

Mark's spirit remained troubled as only one time before. *When was that?* He worked his memory, until it came back. It was the first battle with the Viking Berserkers. During that fight he remembered the darkness of their eyes and the intensity of their fighting. The Berserkers were compelled with energies much stronger than amplified human motivations. There had been a *different worldliness* about the battle. Mark understood that Erik had that same capacity, and if he was also a trainer of men, he would be much more dangerous.

> Those who give to the next generation have the most forceful impact. They must hone their training into its essential foundation principles and master them.

Those who give to the next generation have the most forceful impact. They must hone their training into its essential foundation principles and master them. Generation-trainers must teach in pure ways; then the disciple will be engraved with the extract of the lessons they are taught. This sort of disciple receives the living substance of the teaching, not just the principles. They become purebloods of the discipline. When you deal with a pureblood disciple, you do not encounter the principle of the teaching, you meet the reality.

If Erik is a disciple maker, he will be doubly difficult to defeat, especially if he was discipling them in evil ways.

Erik was a pureblood of rebellion. He would not be dismissed by reason or mercy. Those he trained would multiply his own ability and the pain in his heart would become a devilish furnace. Mark knew this in his spirit, and whispered, "He will come back, and try to kill me." Mark prayed. He fell asleep trusting the Lord.

# Chapter Seven

# BERSERKERS AGAIN

"He trains my hands for war" (Psalm 18:34).

The year ended with the entrance of a great winter storm. The history-making blizzard continued unabated for weeks beyond the normal winter dates and the deep cold remained beyond the opening of Spring. The snow, wind, and cold stacked up ice on the northern coasts. Harbors were clogged with wagon-sized ice-blocks. These huge ice-forms stretched out into the ocean currents, prohibiting any safe sea travel. The fisherman and farmers referred to it as a this-has-never-happened-before kind of winter.

Inland, the snow was several feet deep for two months, and almost every household lost livestock. The cattle and horses were hardy, but the persistent hammering of the cold wore down the animals, and the losses mounted. Although the king's livestock had a greater survival rate due to warmer barns, even he lost cattle and two of his favorite royal horses.

Spring entered on a delayed schedule and the stories about the cold weather began to come from traders. They confirmed the storm had blanketed Germanic regions and the Frankish empire. In the weeks ahead, even more reports relayed the plague-like cold in the northern part of the world. One man told of animals frozen in a region of the Slavs. The violent wind and hard cold had frozen them in standing positions. The villagers could not believe this story until it was heard three times with the last testimony coming from a man who had seen some of the frozen animals.

As strongly as the cold came and as slowly as it left, the late arriving spring was refreshing and vibrant with life. The trees and flowers came back as if trying to make up for lost time. The colors were vivid and bright. All of creation was alive and bursting forth with a majestic freshness. The farmers rejoiced at the miraculous productivity in their livestock. The cattle bore healthy calves at a multiplied rate. Those who lost many animals said two years later all the losses had been regained with more added.

The singing at church was full of joy. The church gatherings were filled with rejoicing hearts every Sabbath. Prayer times were electrified with the nearness of the Spirit of God and a glad 'fear of Him' settled on hearts. Never before had the area been so alive with love and genuine unity. The community was invigorated. A kind of resurrection had come into the hearts of the people. They loved each other, and each one testified to a supernatural peace in the air. No one knew how to explain it, but the whole region was filled with exuberance, and the town plaza was often bubbling with pleasant conversations and helpful considerations. Serving each other was done with sincere hearts, and the people easily preferred others over themselves. All knew something different was happening, and even "ungodly" people understood it was a blessing from the

Lord. Although none knew why it was happening, that entire region of the king's realm enjoyed the blessing and thanked the Lord often for sending it.

There were the rare moments of disagreement, but they were resolved quickly. It was as if the Lord had come to town and was changing all who lived there. Merchants passing through commented on it most every day. That summer was like heaven on earth.

But when autumn arrived, a dark intrusion came—not from inside the people, but as a threat against the land. News had come that Berserkers were planning an invasion. The king heard an account from a member of his Royal Blue Guard who had been sent to search out the Vikings to the Northeast. Everyone knew it was essential to guard the borders and these royal watchers were assigned distant duty beyond the edges of Saxon land to discover any pending threats.

Every nation has borders. These must be recognized, honored, and secured effectively. Even children understood that. No nation is stable if the borders of the land are not defined and guarded. A man's home has borders as does his property. This was one of the rudimentary pillars of social relationship. Governments not honoring the borders of geography and personal property have always been judged as oppressive by history's pen.

The idea of a trespass is built on the necessity of the borders being clearly recognized between people in all manner of social interaction. Such concepts need no extra thought. They simply must be affirmed. They are self-evident. At the most basic levels of community is the understanding of defined and protected territories. The unity and joy-filled momentum of that summer was now quickly turned toward discovering what would be the best strategy to thwart the anticipated invasion.

The king's agent overheard the information being shared between two Norse commanders. They were sitting at a corner table in a tavern and thought no one could hear them. Truly, one of the downsides of consuming alcohol is the unnoticed diminishing of judgment and loss of accuracy in perception. Thinking no one could hear due to the noise of the place, their conversation was still overheard. Though speaking in hushed tones, their efforts did not prevent the man at the next table from hearing.

For an hour, they discussed the planned invasion against the Saxons. They remarked that it was set for early in the harvest season before the days became too cold and while the people would be intent on reaping the abundant crops. The Royal Guard agent played his role perfectly and heard perfectly. The two, dulled by alcohol, had no idea they had betrayed their nation.

The agent was in that place at that time by the grace of God; the Viking's scheme of war was underway. The overheard conversation was verified the next morning, when the agent saw large stands of supplies being assembled near the port as if some excursion was in the offing. The agent knew he must hasten his return to King Egbert. He arranged with the fisherman who had brought him, to take him back early. He complained to the fisherman of some *dis-ease* in his stomach and the need to cut his trip short. The man with the boat had no problem changing plans. They left the next morning, and the secret information was carried to King Egbert.

When the king heard the report, the preparations and implementation of strategies in response to this information were discussed in governing circles. These secret gatherings were marked by the unity formed during the summer's blessings from God. The entire realm had come under this blessing. The wise of heart concluded the blessing God had sent in the previous season was provided so this invasion did not overwhelm them. That recent blessing was forging a fresh honor within the kingdom.

Within the castle community, the urgent preparation for military action was well-known, yet discreetly managed. That prospect did not paralyze or intimidate them; instead, it enabled them to pray, prepare and stand together. The supernatural unity fleshed out a new discretion to keep the information close and not divulge it through dulled perceptions. The story of how the agent got the information was known by the Blue Guard, and it steeled them to maintain decorum and not betray their land.

After summits of prayer were conducted and wise counsel exchanged, it was agreed the Saxons would launch a pre-emptive strike on the Norsemen's key southernmost coastal stronghold. This would not be an invasion to take the Vikings land. Instead, they wanted to send a firm message: "Stay away from us!" The Viking camp was the strategic location for their defense and the embarkation point for offensive efforts. It was situated on a peninsula jutting out directly southward into the sea.

The Saxons recognized this target as the decisive point for

halting the Viking's invasion. The plan must be bold, and it required precise timing since surprise was a critical component of their assault. It was decided to use the Viking boats, which were left on the shore from the Berserker's invasion years before. These had been stored in a secured barn where they were dry and in excellent shape. There were 30 small craft that would be used in a camouflaged action. The Saxon's make-shift armada would arrive from the south. The men in these boats would be appareled as Vikings, but each Saxon warrior had a small red cloth sewn into the right shoulder. The red cloth would identify their side in any battle action, lest their Viking garments confuse them in any fighting. This group of 30 boats would be part of the initial group of warriors. The raid would begin at dawn.

However, the 30 would be preceded by a much smaller boat. This small boat would carry six rowers and four warriors. This one small craft was the point of the spear for their preemptive strike. If the four warriors in the first boat did not fulfill their assignment, the essential element of surprise would be lost. Mark was in that first boat. He was the finest warrior they had. This first boat must dismiss the sentries who would be on guard. The timing for taking out those watchmen on the peninsula had to be accomplished in the minutes just before sunrise or the plan and its necessary surprise element could fail.

The main wave of 30 ships could take the south-facing beach, but only after the first boat's four warriors had taken out the camp's watch-guards. The last phase involved a larger group of fishing boats, which would be filled with several hundred armed and ready men. These would provide additional support for the attack and protect the return to Saxon territory after the stronghold had been secured.

The move was audacious. The Saxons prayed for a blessing from the Lord on this preharvest assault. The timing for the invasion was set 10 days before the Vikings were planning their attack.

Strategically, the Saxons had established their attack to synchronize with one of the Viking's annual celebrations. This festival centered on their worship of Odin, the chief of the Norsemen's panoply of gods. The Saxons chose the last day of the Viking's three-day festival to attack. The feast was celebrated during the autumn equinox, and the worship consisted of rituals with blood sacrifice and meals washed down with copious amounts of mead, an alcoholic mix of honey, water and fruit. The Saxon leaders aptly believed the Norsemen would be numbed by large amounts of alcohol in their bodies and brains. At the end of this three-day feast, they expected to overrun them with more efficiency since they would be compromised physically and mentally.

The Vikings celebrated in the typical manner of idolatrous affairs. Whatever the specific rituals were, for most of the soldiers, the festival did not typically include an authentic loyalty to Odin himself. Most idol worshipers are not genuinely loyal to their god, they participate in the rituals because of tradition or they loved the carnal pleasures associated with the festival. The event was anticipated because it was an opportunity to indulge themselves with no restrictions.

Normally the chief of the Vikings would solicit women to come and 'worship' with the men. For them, the alcohol and the women were the main attraction, not Odin. With the lush supply of food and free-flowing drink, any previous ethical limitations or self-control would be gladly ignored. The disciplines forming military readiness would not be as sharp. The necessary heart-strength to enter battle would not be strong.

The Viking stronghold was situated in a naturally formed topographic 'bowl' with a great level field in the center. There was a road stretching back inland to the north, and it reached to the interior of their nation. Initially, that lane had been scratched through a stand of mixed trees. While it was straight enough to allow supplies to come in easily, it had been intentionally built with occasional curves and mounded hills of rock and dirt, so that in the event of a retreat, the invaders could not advance at a quick pace lest they be ambushed at a bend in the road. It was perfect.

If the Saxons were to take this stronghold, they must face great geographic opponents. The first were the two ridges that framed the level field in this picturesque 'bowl.' These ridges were directly to the west and east. Both were beautifully covered with luxuriant grass, but they were not symmetrical. The east ridge extended abruptly from the flat center of the bowl; it went skyward over 200 feet at a severe angle, then plummeted straight down a rock cliff into the sea. The solid rock walls stood staunchly against any invasion plan, and because there was no beach, the harsh waves would mercilessly crash any sea vessel against the cliff. Attempting to stabilize an assault from that side would be impossible. The Vikings did not bother to guard it. To attack from the sunrise side was not an option and would be deadly to anyone foolish enough to try it.

To attempt a direct assault and land on the beach from the south in open water would also be unwise since the attacking force could be easily observed from a distance. The element of surprise was necessary for the plan to be successful, and a watched sea would not allow that. Only if the sentries could be eliminated would the group of 30 boats have an unobserved approach. From the middle of the peninsula, the watchmen were granted an unhindered view with clear sight lines in three directions, providing a marvelous position for the defense of their camp.

The western side was the only possible avenue for an assaulting force to draw near without being seen. Yet, that too, appeared unassailable.

From inside the camp the western ridge, unlike the eastern one, rose gracefully from the floor of the bowl's natural plaza. Its' slope was not as severe as the steep ascent on the east. The west was veneered with lush green grass that could withstand the harsh weather and was situated like a Roman coliseum's seating arrangement. It was angled upward in a lovely symmetrical curve. It was beautiful and as lovely as an artist's rendition for a pastoral mosaic. But the beauty of the site, as inviting as it was, was not the concern of the Saxons.

There were barriers they must overcome on the west side and they were harsh indeed. Any effort to reach the top of that picturesque western hillside involved pressing through three dangerous concerns. Before anyone could be positioned on that ridge overlooking the camp, those three great difficulties had to be conquered. Just one of them would have been an effective wall to defend the camp. In combination, the three were like an iron wall, refusing entrance.

But there was no other option. Complaining about the three barriers would not lessen the hardships that must be engaged. After the four warriors landed on the flat, sandy beach that bordered the western shore, they would cross a short space peppered with small scrubby trees. These small woody forms were the ugly 'foyer' into the horrific trio of barriers.

Immediately following the short trees, was the first trial: It was a 200-yard maze of massive boulders clumped in disarray; they were strewn about as if flung by some giant hand. These boulders presented themselves as a small mountain range. This field of boulders could not be circumnavigated. The huge uneven stones were 5 to 8-feet tall and spaced with gaps wide enough apart to prevent jumping safely from one boulder top to another. It would not be reasonable to meander through the field. Going around the boulders on foot could be a waste of valuable time.

In the predawn darkness, much time would be lost trying to find a path that might still lead to a dead end. Losing their sense of direction would be easy in the dark. They would be navigating a maze blindly. The height and awkward sizes of these huge stones forced them to climb up one and then climb down. Then they would have to do it again; it would be an exhausting and rigorous effort.

Beyond the field of boulders was the second barrier: a steeply inclined hill. The incline was much worsened by a congregation of barbed trees, choking any route up the slope. The branches were decorated with 2 to 3-inch thorns. These organic barbs were more than able to pierce leather, skin, and muscle. The stand of trees, like the boulders, did not allow them any path around. The army of trees would have to be penetrated, even though they were tightly united and stood as an impervious armor. The trek through the trees would be a torture chamber. It was 60 yards long and would seem like a mile to traverse.

This shorter distance than the boulder-field would still be unavoidably painful. A man the size of Mark would endure the worst treatment from the countless piercings of these thorn trees. It would be like hundreds of bee stings or knife-wounds were received before the third and final barrier was reached.

The last obstacle was the most daunting: another rock cliff. The height was not as elevated as the eastside behemoth, nor was the angle as vertical. The face of it supplied a few scattered hand and foot holds, but in the early morning lack of light, it would be dangerous. Adding the darkness and the fatigue of the prior two obstacles, it was a formidable mountain. The fact was that just one of this trio of earth-based barriers presented an overwhelming threat to success.

The site was perfect for the Vikings and secured them in every way. The site was horrible for the Saxons and opposed them in every way.

The Viking camp was arranged inside this beautiful bowl with two major buildings. One was a large wooden structure that served as the hub of the camp and could comfortably accommodate 500 men. It was structured around a very tall and thick oak tree that had been trimmed and served as the support for the roof and walls. It was an 'organic' edifice that served as the practical and social center of the camp. Whether staging a war or worshiping the idol god, Odin, it was the living hub of the Viking stronghold. There were some smaller huts used for storage of weapons, food, and various supplies. These were sparsely spread among the scores of tents for the men.

Off to the right, as you looked at the camp from the sea, was the commander's quarters. It was a veritable fortress that housed the leader and perhaps 30 of his best warriors. The four corners of this strong structure were solidified by large stones mortared together. Then, massive, heavy oak beams were cut and grooved together to erect the walls. These would stand against every enemy onslaught. Its structural strength was impenetrable.

The Saxon's assault strategy sequence had specific objectives. First, the small boat carrying the four best warriors would land on the western side of the peninsula under the cover of darkness, before midnight. They must arrive at the top of the western side of the camp before sunrise. Their task was to take out the sentries who were on watch. They anticipated 6 to 10 men would be on guard. With the anticipated celebration of Odin concluded and the warriors in less than optimum fighting status, there would still be sentries on lookout.

The four stout warriors expected the Viking sentries would focus their attention to the south, not the east or west, since the land had its own nature-formed walls of defense. With that confidence, the four believed they could gain the ridgetop unobserved and remove the sentries with their arrows. The guards would only be watching the sea.

After the watchmen were removed, that group of four would light a signal fire to give notice for the second wave made up of the 30 boats to hit the beach. These would land on the beach and attack the assembly hall with its groggy men and the commander's quarters with its not-so-groggy men.

Then, the group of fishing boats with several hundred men, would come after the initial wave of 30 to establish the beachhead and provide cover for the withdrawal. The Saxons expected to win the day. The strike was set to occur just before dawn. They only wanted to send the message to stay away and then go back to their homes. This was not an invasion; it was a preventive, pre-emptive strike.

The quartet of first-rank soldiers in the small craft included Mark, Galvin, Edward and a man named Maxim. He was the shortest of the four, but he was built like a tree stump with limbs of iron. Maxim's shoulders and arms were able to exert tremendous force. He had squeezed and broken an oaken keg with his bare hands. As the elite archer of the kingdom, he had struck three melons with three separate arrows from 350 yards. This time, the distance his arrows must travel from the ridge to the center of the camp was no more than 250 yards. It should not be a problem for him. In addition, Galvin and Edward had become skilled with the longbow. The plan was for the three archers with longbows to provide the aerial support.

93

The small armada of Saxons left their families and homes early enough to assemble three days before the ships would embark. The first small boat would leave and travel to the peninsula's west coast. This smaller Viking boat with Mark and his brothers would travel with a group of 10 average fishing boats. The small warship with the four was concealed in that group of 10.

Early morning on the second day before the attack, the 10 boats and the boat with the four left. The group of 30 would leave later that day. They all sailed and rowed with favorable winds. The 10 fishing boats, accompanying the smaller craft, would back away just before the coast of the peninsula was sighted. This allowed the four-man team to advance in the dimming light of dusk. The six rowers glided silently to the intended shore. The night was moonless, the stars brilliant and the sea waves barely troubled.

When the boat was secured on the small shore, they estimated they had five hours until pre-dawn sunlight would brighten the world too much to be unnoticed. The wind speed increased slightly. They thought, *"No threat with that,"* at least not yet. The six rowers stayed with the boat. The four gathered up the weapons and tools they needed to overcome the barriers and closed the distance to the first hindrance of the three obstacles, the field of boulders.

The boulders were even larger than they had expected and were tilted at strange angles. Most were taller than Mark, and they were also rimmed with sharp, uneven edges. To avoid cutting their hands, several minutes were spent tearing up two shirts to wrap their palms and fingers. The routine of climbing up one boulder, then getting down and climbing the next was exhausting. All four of them fell off boulders more than once due to the slippery stones. Maxim fell off the same rock three times. Traversing the large field of massive stones took less than two hours, but they were already behind schedule.

After the effort expended to cross the boulder field, all four were sweating profusely and breathing hard. They came to the inclined tree line, which rose so severely, they had to lift their knees above their waists to take the next step. Every move forward involved passing through thickly pressed trees with thorny branches that cut, scraped, and pierced their limbs and face. Mark understood why the Vikings saw no need to watch this side of their encampment, guarded as it was by hundreds of barbed sentinels.

Mark remembered his father's wisdom in the pressure places of life. James taught him that answers, success, miracles, and progress are frequently surrounded by problems. You can either quit or press through them. If you quit, you join the ranks of the majority. The pressures you overcome are what God uses to build strength into you, just as the hammer and fire build strength into the swords you make. Mark could hear his dad's steady voice inside. He encouraged his heart, mind, and body to address the slope of thorns.

> ... answers, success, miracles, and progress are frequently surrounded by problems.

The four patiently pressed into the pain and agony of the

climb—in silence, except for the involuntary groans that were expelled as they climbed into the pain. This was necessary, so they did it. This was torture. Once they stepped into the tree line, any move in any direction was horribly painful. The four of them were bleeding from hundreds of piercings in a few moments. Each of them had to stop every few steps to brace themselves forward.

They now found themselves even farther behind schedule. The wind was slowly growing stronger. Although it was dark, the sky seemed to be growing even darker. *"How could that be since dawn was drawing near?"*

The distance they had to walk was not that long laterally, but the inclined angle was increasing, necessitating twice as many steps. The breathing of these hardy men was hoarse and the gasps for air were sliced with grunts of pain. Their steps were slowing. Each man's hands, arms, neck, and legs were bleeding from multiple cuts. Twice Mark became stuck between trees and had to force his body into the thorns to go forward. Still, they all knew what was ahead. The cliff had yet to be conquered. Mark recalled how fatiguing the training had been under Sir John, but none of that was as difficult as this.

Then, after they had finally cleared the trees of pain, all four desperately needed a break because they were bleeding from multiple wounds. They stopped. But the dawn was approaching more quickly than planned for and the wind was stronger and increasingly intense. Now they stood at the base of the 70-foot cliff. The indicators of dawn revealed what the accelerating winds were bringing. Large, dark, and heavy clouds were moving quickly and racing toward them from the west—ominous and billowing! The wind was becoming raucous and violent. The rain had not started, but they could see it in the distance. The cliff remained unchanged, continuing to challenge them.

Four strong, bleeding men stopped … to breathe … to think … to pray … and to complete the task that would position them to start their purpose. The effort they had exerted to this point was more than most would express in reaching a final goal. For the four, the fighting had not begun yet, and the storm would arrive any moment.

Maxim came up with an idea. He saw how to ascend this nearly straight-up cliff. There were a few hand and foot holds formed by erosion spaced on its face. Standing could be accomplished on those slightly level spots. Maxim studied the cliff's façade carefully and prepared a pathway in his mind. Next, he tied a small but strong rope to a thicker oak-shafted arrow. He backed up a few feet, fitted the arrow and aimed it into a hollow 20 feet up the wall. The hollow was above a small ledge. Mark, Galvin, and Edward were not sure of his plan, so they watched and waited.

The rope would drag the arrow's flight downward, so Maxim pulled the bow back as if he were shooting it hundreds of yards. The three wondered, *"What is this?"* Even in the dim light the stormy predawn was providing, Maxim's aim was true and on target. The arrow disappeared into the hole with the rope rapidly following until it stopped. Maxim smiled and with a hope based on his faith in the Lord, began to slowly pull the rope expecting something inside the hollow would stop the arrow and pull back. With his third pull, the rope stopped at the entrance of the hole and the arrow turned lengthwise. Maxim pulled harder. There was no further movement. He pulled very hard, but the rope remained locked in place.

With no comment, he picked up a sharp-edged rock, and began to climb the cliff to that small ledge. There was 50 feet remaining. The three were impressed, but they said nothing. The arrow and rope had created a beginning and Maxim was making a trail for them up the cliff. He secured the rope for the other three to climb.

Then, his next shot, with the same arrow, would be more difficult because standing on the narrow ledge was a challenge, but the target was easier due to the V-shaped formation of the stone. He accomplished his shot in the accelerating winds and the dawning of the day. Now the first two ropes for the three to climb up were knotted into place.

The final arrow would travel a shorter distance, and Maxim took the sharp, jagged stone and tied it to the rope to make sure it caught on something after he shot. The problem was there was no way to see a place to secure it. The wind was increasing, the sun's brim was about to break the edge of the eastern horizon. Maxim prayed, "O God, You Who hold all things together, cause this stone to get stuck onto a root at the top of this hill!"

He fired the stone-laden arrow over the ridge's edge and waited for the rope to drop from its flight. It landed in a spot unseen. He began to pull the rope. He pulled again and then ... it stuck. He pulled hard ... it moved a bit and then, it stuck ... hard. Maxim climbed up. The stone was stuck on the root of a tree, and he thanked the Lord for answering his prayer.

The three climbed up, and in a few moments three archers and a large man stood together just below the eastern ridge. As the sun was breaking the day open in the east, and the dark clouds were blackening the sky from the west, the men were ready to take out the sentries. The wind was strong, howling, and harsh ... the first large drops of rain fell, heavy, angled by the winds. The four stood in the initial rainfall. The drops stung: pouring over their deeply scratched bodies. The stinging water served to wake up and invigorated them. It washed the blood off. They were being energized by the stinging rain.

Silently, the high four positioned themselves just below the top of the ridge. They stood below the ridge top to prevent any of the guards from seeing their erect profiles above the ridgeline.

In the bowl below, six men served as sentries. They had missed the last night of the idol-celebration because of lapses in military conduct. They were assigned to the watch as a discipline. None of them were happy about missing the last night, but the rising storm was prompting a fresh alertness. The sentries were on the floor of the bowl-shaped field. They were unaware they were being watched by eight eyes peering down from the west. The six were now alert because the storm was growing in its fury, but their eyes were especially intent on the sea.

The four positioned themselves near the top of the ridge and were ready to initiate the plan. Maxim gained his target and stretched the bow with the first arrow. He was ready to let it loose when Mark raised his hand to halt him. The wind, the rain, the lightning, and thunder were cascading down. The high four were still watching, waiting on Mark's order. The low six were anxious, aware of the storm, but not of the battle's beginning. Two of the six suddenly went to the assembly hall to give a report and get orders. The remaining low four waited for the increasing storm. They were very awake.

The 30 Viking ships manned by the Saxons were offshore, going up and down in the storm's waves. They were looking for the signal to take the beach. The storm was assisting in keeping them hidden from view, but the waves were rough. The signal fire had not been lit for them to move in. Indeed, how would they be able to start the fire in this driving rain? The challenges kept mounting.

None of them imagined what happened next. Among the Berserker's list of gods was Thor, the god of thunder. But thunder only exists because lightning goes first. The true God of the lightning spoke first, and it was before the thunder-god could do anything.

As the two from the six approached the assembly place which was filled with deeply sleeping and drunk-deadened men, a massively bright lightning blast struck the assembly room's tree-pillar and set it ablaze with a majestic bolt! The entire area shuddered. The charge of light traveled down the main trunk of the hall and exploded at the base, killing four men asleep on the ground. The two sentries going to the hall for orders were thrown backwards by the heavenly shaft of light.

The surprise the Saxons wanted came from a different source all together. The signal fire came from a different source, too.

All were startled awake to a fear-filled consciousness. Mark shouted to Maxim, "Shoot the arrow!" Maxim let it go and in less than three seconds, a man who did not know it was his last day, left this life with no idea how or why he had departed. Before that man had fallen, Galvin and Edward let their first arrows go, and two more followed their fellow soldier into eternity. The fire set by God signaled the other boats to come, and they came with no hesitation. The chief over these boats mused ... *"Quite an impressive signal fire."*

The commander's tent had no drunken men in it. It is not wise for leaders to be drunk, and this leader was no fool. His men were not groggy—the bolt had awakened them to their full capacities. They were the best in the camp. For this commander, the storm was simply a naturally occurring phenomena— something they dealt with on a regular basis. Storms were no problem for those who worshiped the god of thunder. But this bolt from the true God would dramatically adjust the commander's theology.

The four above on the ridge had one more guard to take out. Maxim eliminated him. As Mark, Galvin and Edward rushed down the hill toward the camp, the rain had washed all the blood from their thorn-pricked bodies. They were clean and refreshed. They were completely alert.

Soon, the Saxon boats, accelerated by the wind, would quickly reach the small sandy beach. But, the Norsemen, dulled by their drunkenness, would be ill-prepared to fight. They had been expelled from their tents by the fire ignited by God's bolt. They were not alert in the chaos, and they were ignorant of the approaching boats and the four dead sentries. They still thought it was just a storm with an unexpected fire. Sleepy soldiers sought to put out the fire started by God.

This divine distraction was helpful to disguise the arrival of the 30 boats. The Viking chief, however, discerned the attack quickly. He saw the Saxon boats arrive. The boats were ejecting men prepared to protect their homeland from invasion.

The dark storm forced its winds and rain on the stronghold from the west. The sun was shining brilliantly from the east. Dark clouds burdened with torrential downpours were driven sideways by southwesterly gales. Those heavy and dark cloud-waterfalls were prismed by brilliant sunrays from the east, like converging extremes, colliding in the skies. Two forces, heavenly and earthly met on that finger of land. Mark knew this was more than a physical battle—it was a fight between darkness and light. Then he noticed a brilliant rainbow began to form over the chaotic battlefield, a rainbow in the rain—a sign in the storm.

Two groups merged in crazy disorder. The Berserkers were yelling from the demonized source of their power. Their grogginess was being replaced by an evil rage; but first, several were taken down by the ordered hearts of the God-fearing men. The chief stood outside the door of his fortress and took in the scene, barking orders in the storm. He was a man of power, unintimidated by this surprise attack. He began to ferociously assault the Saxon men. He was effective. Mark saw him and moved immediately with a focused gaze through the field of fighters to face the Viking chief.

Maxim had taken out the fourth guard and was running down the hill to join the others, when he stopped suddenly. He realized his elevated position afforded a strategic overview, from which he could serve his fellow warriors. He had 15 arrows left. Maxim would join the weather and rain down arrows of death from his high ground. He pulled the arrows out and placed them next to his feet. He took aim at strategic opponents and saved several Saxon soldiers that day with 14 long-distance shots. He reserved his 15th for the chief.

Mark had arrived to face the leader of the Viking stronghold. Establishing his feet, he caught the chief's eyes. No words were exchanged, as they simultaneously locked into deep appraisals. They were assessing and recognized each other as the primary. This ability to rapidly discern the capability or intent of a man was essential to being an effective leader in battle. If a leader could not determine who was a legitimate threat quickly, he simply would not survive. The winds whirled and the rain came in angry torrents. Both men knew the other was formidable; a sense of destiny overshadowed the field as they faced off. One of them would die.

The images of that day were deeply etched into the minds of all who were there. A bizarre mechanism generated a strange phenomenon. As Mark and the Viking leader squared off, both sides ceased fighting to watch them. Each group recognized these two were the best. Unconsciously, the warriors from both sides circled to form a human theater. The two sides would watch. The thought … *"Let us see what our best warrior can do,"* unified both sides.

Neither Mark nor the chief gave heed to their audience. This was not a contest. It was not practice. A strange fear came upon all of them, as a palpable soundlessness descended over the field.[1] The wind and the rain pulled back. The lightning flashed overhead one more time and with it came the kind of thunder you feel in your bones. At that instant, the Viking chief propelled a vicious and speedy thrust. He had killed many with this singular move, but this time, his sword pierced only the air. He smiled at Mark's agility and mused, *"Finally, I meet a man worth killing."*

Mark waited, looking for the right time to strike. An experienced swordsman has unique moves and skills. Each warrior's style has been honed by thousands of hours of training and war. A seasoned warrior develops specific ways to fight. Mark knew he could not be lazy. He knew he could not make an error with this man. This was the fiercest warrior he had ever met—his match—in every way, but one. Mark stood as if unfazed by the man's speed; yet inwardly, he was impressed. He had never fought someone with this kind of skill, focused, fearless, and demonized. *"How do you intimidate a man who is not afraid to die?"* he thought.

Both were positioning for mastery. And because their first maneuverings were more defensive, the fight went on several

---

[1.] There are numerous historic accounts from war stories when an entire field of battle was charged with frenzy or stillness. The men, who have survived such a moment, describe it as a strange atmosphere. Some would call it an entrance of demons; others spoke of it as divine. But it would come over both sides.

moments with no advantage gained by either one. The scene was stretching out longer than the Vikings liked. They realized Mark was also a champion, and the Vikings were worried for their chief. They were growing impatient with the ongoing positioning.

Mark had stepped back due to an especially harsh swing by the Viking, and he was now closer to the Berserker's side of the theater. One of the Vikings at Mark's back set himself to strike Mark from his blindside. The man considered it, and then raised his blade to pierce Mark's heart from behind.

Instead, the stillness was sliced with the strange sound of a long swift swoosh and thump! Maxim's 15th arrow thudded into the man's heart. He fell forward, then, everyone stopped and turned to discover Maxim 200 yards away on the hill. He waved as if to say, "You can proceed now, but do it fairly." He could not let them know he had no more arrows.

Mark had noticed a small flaw in the chief's defense when he swung his blade left to right across his body. Mark also recognized a slowing in the man's reactions. He was tiring. The chief had never fought a man like Mark. He was becoming desperate. His concentration was flagging. Then with a heretofore uncharacteristic impulsiveness, the Viking lunged, missed, and swung left to right. Mark saw the opening, and in a flash, his sword was inserted in the flaw of his defense—he struck the chief deeply in the midsection. The Viking remained standing, but all in the theater knew it was a fatal piercing. He would be dead in moments.

The stillness was shattered by a demonic screeching rage

on one side, and a joy-filled shouting on the other. The theater collapsed on each other in a furious cataclysm of violence.

No one noticed the storm had stopped and that the boats with 300 Saxons had arrived, and soon, the Berserkers began to forfeit their stronghold to the flood of Saxons overwhelming their position. The Viking's first efforts had been fierce and strong, but the death of their Chief and the alcoholic impact was quickly reducing their normal endurance and courage. The fact is that idols have no ultimate energy against the true God. The Vikings began to retreat inland. For the Norsemen, the day had grown bitter. Their commander, a great warrior had fallen to the Saxon's best—this defeat would haunt them. The Saxons did not pursue them. Their point had been made.

When the Berserkers fled, they left their leader on the ground. Mark knew they would return for his body. He went over to the fallen chief. He brought one of his men who understood the language of the Vikings. The chief was in evident pain and struggling. He was still breathing and desperately aware of his near death. Most others would have already given up, but this dying warrior still had the spark of life in his heart. Mark knelt over the Norse chief, and with the translator's help, spoke, "You are a great warrior."

The Viking's eyes brightened; his head nodded slightly. "You have served your god with all you heart, but here at death's door, you have no hope. Your heart has no peace for what you are about to face," Mark remarked, and he allowed that statement to sink into the chief.

"The God we love is the one true God. He is the Creator of

all. There is no god like Him! He judges all things rightly."

The Viking leader was listening, amazed the man who pierced him was speaking in this authoritative and peace-filled voice. The chief mused, *"These are such strange words, but, why this passion and compassion?"*

Mark continued, "The true God, the Lord of heaven and earth, sent His son, Jesus to die for our sins and receive us as His own children. He conquered death for us. He has an amazing love for every person, and He also has this love for you. You are about to die, but you may call on Him. If you are willing, He will hear you." After a short pause, Mark asked, "May I pray to my God for you?"

The Viking warrior was stunned. *"Who is this man? Why does he care?"* The great chief closed his eyes, thinking, considering this unusual day and this unusual man, slowly, he opened his eyes, and nodded.

Mark laid his hand on the man's chest and prayed, "Great God of heaven, the Lord of every man in all the earth, thank You for sending Jesus. Thank You for opening the eyes of our hearts to see and know You. Would You have mercy on this man, this warrior, and reveal Yourself to him in these, his last moments? in Jesus' name." Mark smiled with the countenance of an angel, stood up and positioned the man in a more comfortable pose and walked away.

The Viking chief lay there, as his life blood was flowing out. He was in a great quandary. Something had happened to him as the other man prayed. Some sort of unearthly peace had come over him that was not physical. In his mind, he had sensed a power working in him during the prayer—both eerie and easing. A new kind of courage stood up in him at death's door. Then he coarsely whispered to the God the man had prayed to, "This man of Yours, he knows You. If You are who he says You are, let me see You with my heart too." He closed his eyes. He departed his body moments later with a smile on his face. He had not smiled since childhood.

Mark walked over to other wounded Vikings lying on the field. They would survive because the Saxons did not desire to kill them. The Saxons bandaged many of the Viking wounded as if they were their own men. Mark communicated to these Viking warriors, especially those who were part of the chief's inner circle. "We heard about your plans to invade our land because two of your leaders were sloppy in their talk at a tavern. They betrayed your people," Mark told them. "We do not want to invade your land. We honor what the God of heaven and earth has given you for your land. We did this to let you know we will defend our land, and we ask you to respect us in the same manner."

The Saxon soldiers finished tending to their own wounded and wrapped up their five dead soldiers to take home. Then all the warriors knelt before the Lord, thanked Him for His grace in the stormy battle and asked for mercy on the journey home.

# Chapter Eight

# ROUND TWO WITH ERIK—OPEN HEAVENS & DEATH'S DOOR

"Fools, because of their transgression, and their
iniquities, were afflicted. He sent His word and
healed them" (Psalm 107:17).

The next season broke fresh and clean after the return of the
sailor-soldiers from the assault against the Vikings. The threat
of their invasion had been pushed back, and the year since
then had been laced with the continued blessings, which had
preceded the news of the planned invasion.

The family, the community, and the king's realm were all
experiencing an invigorating newness. Truly, springtime filled
everyone's heart. Families told of changes in their children.
Rebellious young men were softening and submitting gladly
to their parents. Fathers were asking their children to forgive
them for their angry words and harsh discipline. Husbands
and wives, who had spent years in constant quarreling, were
humbling themselves one to the other and choosing to become
kind and gracious households.

Ten months after the fight with Erik, one of the strangest

and yet most wonderful things occurred. There was a report from a man whose last name was Smithson. He told a friend that Erik had changed for the better. The friend did not believe it, so the report did not spread very far. But over the next few weeks, as testimonies came about God's blessing here and there in the far stretches of the realm, others also brought news that Erik had changed. They told how his attitude and actions had dramatically adjusted for the better. He was serving and helping people.

Most who knew him did not believe it. Yet, over time, it was difficult to deny the eyewitnesses to his transformation. People began to include Erik's change of behavior in their thanks to God. The first time he heard that report about Erik, Mark was angry. He did not want God to bless Erik. Mark finally had to admit to himself he was wrong to think that way, but he never spoke to Susanna about the anger or the recognition of his wrong. He kept it inside. *"We will see if this Erik guy has really changed."* Until then, Mark would keep his judgement against Erik and any admission of a bad attitude to himself.

Mark's refusal to thank the Lord with a genuine gratefulness notwithstanding, other reports began to come in from the king's domain. Hundreds of them from the farthest borders of the nation. Whole communities were experiencing miraculous productivity in crops, and the weather was perfect. The rain came at the right time: warm weather came at the right time.

As much as Mark rejoiced over the news of God's blessing in the land, and his own family was awash with that same divine favor, there was a root of bitter resistance that grew more conspicuous each time he heard the news about Erik. He might smile to the person making the comment, but in himself it was rejected.

As a warrior, he was trained to be alert, and something did not fit each time he heard it. One day Susanna asked him a question, as only a wife can penetratingly delve into her husband's heart, "What is going on with you? You are distant." She was not accusing, but she knew something deeper was disturbing him.

Mark hesitated, but then openly confessed, "I am bothered by these testimonies about Erik, and I am bothered about the fact that I am bothered about them. I know I am wrong, and at the same time, I am convinced I am right. My feelings are extreme both ways. I feel convicted for my resistance to the good reports, and yet convinced I'm right."

"The Lord commands us to forgive. We have all been forgiven and did not deserve it. Maybe you ought to do the same," Susanna replied.

Mark was speechless at the simple and direct words. Once again, Susanna had released the Lord's wisdom and revealed His heart.

Over a year had passed since the run-in with Erik. Many reports all said the same thing. Even those who had not liked him before reported Erik was now a delight to be with. "It's a miracle!" was said again and again. Indeed, if Erik had changed, then the heavens must have opened over them. Mark was being convicted for his unforgiving heart.

"Anyway, the fall festival starts in two weeks—it ought to

be a wonderful time with so many people acknowledging this blessing we are all under." Susanna said, as she was seeking to provoke him out of his judging viewpoint. Half-smiling, she added, "Get the log out of your own eye." She was reciting the Lord's admonition to avoid hypocritical pre-judgments against others when we have similar wrongs in ourselves. Mark grinned and set himself to straighten up his attitude.

Mark tried to receive the correction and spent some time trying to rid himself of the high-mindedness. He prayed and spoke words to repent, but He never fully got rid of it, and his two-sided place inside continued to trouble him.

If the heavens were open over the area, they seemed to be closing over Mark. He was not looking forward to the festival even though the whole region was buzzing with anticipation. Susanna's words were right, but still, he couldn't shake it. He prayed again.

Mark delayed going to the festival until the last day. He kept making excuses—he had guard work to do. But he knew he had to attend, because Susanna was the favorite to win the last game of the celebration's competitions. It was just for the ladies. Mark did come on the final day, and he had to admit he always enjoyed watching the game the ladies played at the end of the festival.

Erik had also come for the celebration. He arrived early, several days before. He was in the plaza each day enjoying the fellowship and talking easily with people. He even played with the children. The parents remarked how well he worked with them. All concluded it was true—Erik had changed.

Then the final game was about to begin. A large crowd had moved over to the field where it was always played. Erik was two hundred yards away from the field where the ladies played their game. He was in the market plaza talking to some of the older men in town. They were speaking together of the blessing of the Lord present in recent months. Erik had not yet seen Mark. Mark only came to watch the race.

Since it was a crowd favorite, most everyone loved to watch this last contest. The game was called, 'Hide and Race.' It was played in the large grass field near the forested grounds on the west side of the castle. All the women would line up facing the castle with their backs to the field. Then, one lady would cross the 100 yards long field and hide somewhere inside the tree line of the forest. The other ladies would turn at the signal and try to find the one hiding. If, and or when someone saw the lady hiding, she and the other ladies would race back to the starting line. The last lady there would be the one to hide the next time. Susanna had won that race two years in a row, either because they could not find her, or because she always outran them to the castle.

The game began, and Susanna was first to go and hide. Mark stood with the husbands, brothers, and fathers as they all enjoyed this fun. The ladies lined up and turned their backs to the field. Susanna took off running for the trees. She would conceal herself several yards inside the tree line. Mark watched from the other side of the field and saw her disappear inside the trees. What she did not see was a hooded man who had already picked a place to hide a few yards deeper inside the tree line. He had chosen the right spot. Susanna crouched right in front of his secret pre-decided hiding place. The hood covered most of his face. He had a plan; he was ready. She was not.

Susanna hid behind a large oak. The bushes concealed her completely, but she could still see the field through its branches. Her hiding place was about 30 feet inside the trees. Susanna had worn a brown skirt and top to be less visible. She waited. The signal was sounded, and all the ladies turned to find her.

The hooded man inside the trees moved quietly. Susanna's eyes and full attention were fixed on the field in front of her. The group of ladies was nearing the trees. They were just a few steps from the trees. Suddenly, the hooded one was right behind her; he had a large knife, and he was ready to use it. Susanna sensed his presence and turned around; he had hoped she would. With no warning, he swung the large, sharp knife ... at her face. He intended to draw a line from one cheek at the edge of her mouth to the cheek of the other side. He had practiced it many times. What he did not understand about Susanna was that she was not timid. Although surprised, she still had marvelous reflexes and she ducked in time to avoid being cut across her mouth—the knife's intended target. But she did not duck far enough.

He missed her cheek, but he found her forehead. He swiped a 4-inch scar at her hairline. The wound went to the bone and began immediately to gush blood from the slash. She bled profusely. Susanna screamed. She pushed the man and whirled in terror as she frantically fled toward the field. Mark recognized her voice immediately and moved toward the trees before he saw her. She burst through the tree line covered in crimson.

From a distance Mark saw her face awash with blood. He flew like a falcon descending. The crowd of ladies playing the game saw Susanna break through the trees bleeding, and they turned back quickly toward the starting line in masse. Elizabeth was the only lady who ran toward Susanna at the same time Mark did.

As Mark neared her, he noticed a hooded man running back toward the marketplace. The man had exited the woods quickly, running with a knife. He ran to the left toward the castle plaza. There was a bright white stain on his left boot.

Mark kept an eye on the man even as he grabbed up Susanna. She spewed out her anguish, "He cut me with a knife! I could not see his face! He had a dark red hooded jacket on." She wept in despair, breathing hard and aching from the wound. The skin was laid open to the bone. The scar would remain, but Mark knew she would survive, with a scar.

He continued to watch the knifed man as Susanna collapsed in his arms. "Susanna, you will be okay. Is that the man?" he asked, pointing to the running man.

She looked, "Yes, that's him with the hood."

The man disappeared in the crowd in the plaza. As Elizabeth took up Susanna's care, Mark galloped after the man with the hood. An intense fury formed in him. This was a new anger. Or was it his old anger? Mark did not care. This was a just anger. This time it would be satisfied because this time he had his Longstreet. Whoever the hooded man was, he would pay dearly. Then Mark remembered Erik's threat. Within his first 20 steps, Mark had already concluded it was Erik who had done this. But Mark did not know Erik was standing with the men in the plaza.

The hooded man slowed as he entered the back side of the crowd allowing himself to breathe more easily. He realized Mark was closing on him, but that was also according to his plan. The timing and positioning must be exactly right. He rounded the wagon's end and slipped into a portable shed, unobserved, just behind and out of sight of the circle of men Erik was with. A moment later, Mark roared around the end of the wagon and saw a man's back wearing the very clothes he had seen the man wearing moments ago. The crimson hooded robe and the stain on his left boot convinced Mark. This was the man who had cut Susanna's face with the knife.

"Turn around!" Mark blasted out, his voice like a commander, his Longstreet ready. All the men were startled by the command and looked to Mark. He was positioned for battle in the middle of the festival. Erik turned to meet Mark's eyes. He was surprised at his harsh tone. The history of their contacts raced through Mark's memory as if they all happened yesterday. The bump in the back, the grunted nonspeech, the approach toward Susanna, the simple conversation, the broken wrist, the cut on the chin. This is the same man! Mark's fury rose.

"I knew it was you! You just cut my wife with a knife! You will pay for that now!"

Mark allowed his suspicions to come to the forefront and rejected all the good reports he had heard about Erik having changed. "I do not care what anyone says about you changing," he blurted out. "I know you attacked my wife!"

Everyone nearby was startled, and one of the men who knew Mark spoke up in Erik's defense, "Sir Mark, we are sad to hear of your wife's distress, but Erik has been standing here with us for some time. He could not have done this."

Mark was not willing to hear it. Erik stood silently. He did not defend himself. The old anger from Mark's past stood up and compromised his righteous desire for justice. He would take vengeance on the one who had done the wrong. Mark took his stance for a fight. Because of his anger, Mark's ears had become cloudy, and he could not hear.

Even the elder who had warned him about Erik said, "You should not do this. He is not guilty of your charge against him."

Erik stood still with some surprise because the people were taking a stand for him and against Mark. Even so, Mark's conviction would not be dissuaded. Mark knew in the depths of his bones that Erik had done this. Mark was wrong.

His old anger took the lead and pulsed out like fire from a volcano. "You and I will fight. We will fight now! I challenge you, man to man. I am the friend of the king! You will not refuse me! I will kill you today!"

The crowd was stunned at Mark's use of the king's honor to make this threat. He had waved his ruby-stoned ring with an arrogant and angry confidence. "You attacked my wife. I will not stand by and do nothing!"

Erik stood still, waiting. He knew the dynamics of anger, far better than most. He continued to wait, saying nothing. He would not act to defend himself. Mark

> Impatience coupled with anger is never beneficial.

117

would have to make the first move.

Mark was boiling and anxious to get this fight underway. Impatience coupled with anger is never beneficial. He pushed away the training and self-control he had learned. Then the vision of Susanna's bloodied face crossed his mind's eye. Mark moved suddenly, violently. With a vicious thrust, he intended to impale Erik.

The suddenness of his movement surprised everyone, and the crowd sounded out a united and surprised, "Ohhh..." They were appalled and confused by the violence of this normally gracious man. Mark was sure he would finish this man with one thrust. But Erik was not where Mark's sword went. He had moved. Since Erik knew Mark's anger was ready to strike, he, too, was ready. The fight was started by Mark.

First-time-in-life moments are embossed in the memory for that very reason—they are first-time events. This fight would hold several of them for Mark, and the speed and ease with which Erik dodged his initial stabbing attempt was only one of many first-time surprises. As a result, Mark would recall the flashing of his sword and the skilled brilliance of Erik's knife in vivid detail—excruciatingly painful detail. The fight was underway and was confusing to Mark from the outset. *"Why is it that I cannot outmaneuver a man with a knife?"* thought Mark. The truth was that Mark's rage was mitigating his skills. He was not as effective with his sword when he was angry.

Quickly, the crowd expanded outward and formed another large arena. One man ran to the castle to report to the Blue Guard. Others in this human arena were praying the fight would be avoided or stopped quickly. That prayer request was not answered as desired.

The struggle had begun with a flurry of collisions between the blades. It was fast and then too fast to comprehend as it progressed. Only the clanging of the steel confirmed a real fight was taking place. Those watching could not verify with their eyes what their ears were hearing. Both men moved in and out as artisans would in crafting a masterpiece. Two experts with honed skills displayed remarkable agility, speed, and power. Accelerations from different angles on offence amazed the athletically inclined among the crowd. Then those very skilled expressions were blocked just as splendidly by a coordinated rebuttal from the other fighter. The crowd stood transfixed. Even the four Blue Guards who arrived did not interfere.

Mark was a wonder to watch. How could a man so large move with silky smooth efforts and with an unbelievable forcefulness and speed behind every slashing fling of his sword? His sword sang as it sped through the air and was addictingly eerie to hear.

Erik's knife moved like a flitting butterfly, albeit a butterfly made of iron. His speed matched Mark's. The crowd thought Mark would have the advantage because of the length of his sword; however, Erik's blade parried every blow. He was using his knife in unfathomable ways, and only Mark's extraordinary coordination saved him from death several times. This was the first time Mark had fought a man with a knife. Erik was rapid and unpredictable. He moved closer in toward Mark, and this strategy worked because he crowded and hindered Mark's ability to use the blade fully. Everyone Mark had fought before stepped back from his sword, but not this man. He was fully unintimidated, not afraid to die.

In rapid succession, the sounds came one after the other, fling ... clang ... swish went the knife and the clank of the sword back and forth for several minutes, and still both men were as intense as when they started.

Mark cut Erik's shirtsleeve, but drew no blood. *"His arms are shielded with leather hides up to his neck ... but why?"*

Erik cut Mark's left forearm and blood streamed. Susanna now stood bandaged and concerned at the outside of the circled band of people. Mark swiped low with the Longstreet, and for the first time slightly caught Erik's leg. Despite the crimson flow he seemed unaffected. Erik mounted a swirl of activity like a spinning top. He cut Mark on the first circular spin ... and the second ... and the third.

In this tornado of motions and angles, Mark for the first time in his life was intimidated. Mark's anger was lessening his skills. He found himself hesitating and aware of the four places he was bleeding. They were small cuts, but still.

Susanna began to pray for her husband. Her forehead stung with pain, still oozing blood from under the makeshift bandage, but her heart hurt more than her head. Elizabeth and James held her up and began to pray audibly.

Mark rallied and flipped his sword on its side in mid-swing. He had no intention of cutting Erik. He made a deliberate swipe to strike the knife just above Erik's fist. With a loud clang, the blade flew seven feet in the air and landed near the crowd. Mark relaxed, but Erik casually pulled a knife from the back of his belt and held it this time in his left hand. Mark saw it, shifted his weight on his feet and considered it. Now was another first time for Mark. Erik knew he was troubling the big man.

The four wounds were minor, but Mark knew the longer he fought, the loss of blood would ultimately take its toll on his stamina. He needed to resolve this soon. His heart was strong enough to avenge Susanna for the rest of the day if necessary, but his body was human and subject to weakness.

Mark decided to work in a different style. He had been fighting Erik in a formal and classical way. But suddenly he shifted to a wilder, unpredictable manner, and in three swings he wounded Erik twice. Erik backed up. Mark became beast-like, allowing his anger to control his skills in an ugly manner. He moved with a grotesque fierceness, transforming himself into an unthinking harshness. He no longer cared.

Erik found himself backpedaling and off balance. Erik had confessed he was a new believer, but he was not a mature man of God. He also returned to his basic carnal instincts. Both men were roaring and growling at each other between the strikes of their weapons. The fight was strange: an ugly event expressed from the grossest of motives. Vindictiveness filled the air. The crowd was disgusted with Mark. Indeed, without truly knowing what they were sensing, they could feel the open heavens of blessing being leached out of the town.

Both men were bleeding now, both were weakening, not in their anger, but in the strength to express it. Erik allowed himself to get closer, within range of Mark's blade tip. He held the belt knife in his left hand. He allowed Mark to flip his sword and strike his knife out of his hand a second time. Erik's knife flew to his left on the ground, and Mark again relaxed for a moment.

Although only for an instant, it was long enough for Erik to kneel, grab the third knife from his boot and hurl it into Mark's gut. The blade was shorter, but it went all the way in. Mark fell, more out of surprise, as the strengthless sensation sucked wind from his core. He dropped his sword. *"What just happened?"*

Susanna and Elizabeth shrieked. James tried to move forward to serve his son. Mark fell near Erik's left boot with the whitish stain. With a strange and unintentional focus, Mark found himself staring at the stain on the left boot just inches away from his eyes. With an untimely clarity, he understood the stain had obviously been 'formed' by three fingers. It was clear the three marks were put there on purpose. It was easy to see this close.

Erik was still now, relaxed as he stood over Mark in the way a champion might. This moment of ease proved to be Mark's deliverance from death. Mark raised himself, just a little, to exert a final explosion of life-saving force. He lifted his body on his elbows and twisted to his right, then quickly rocked his weight back to his left, and torqued like a whip on his left elbow and sent his massive right fist into the outside edge of Erik's knee.

Erik's knee broke inwardly with a horrible crunching snap and popping of tendons. The weird sound and the bizarre angle his leg formed, remained an image planted in the minds of those who saw it. They all wished they could forget it. He crumpled with the kind of cries and moans a distressed beast would make. The crowd groaned as Erik savagely twisted on the ground in agony. His howling yelps stuck in the ears the same way the image of the knee snapping stuck in their eyes' memory.

Bleeding profusely, Mark collapsed. He was at death's door. He fainted and continued to bleed. Erik was in extreme pain and kept on screaming as two men came to help him. He was about to pass out. But before he lost consciousness, he saw one last thing—NanLee Smithson's tear-stained face standing a few feet away. She had seen the whole thing and was hurting for him, with rivers of tears. Erik lost consciousness as he gazed at her grief over him. *Why does she care? She doesn't know me.*

The crowd was conflicted and angry, bitter at both men. With anguished hearts, they moved to help them. The two men who came to Erik's side carried him away to get medical attention. James, Elizabeth, and Susanna were the first and most urgent to save Mark's life.

Some of the crowd gathered to give aid, some stood in disbelief, and others walked away with no words to describe the horrible images that had been so perversely planted into them. Dusk settled in on a horribly difficult day. All wondered how they could deal with what happened.

Over an hour later, the wagon with the small shed began to move and then head out of town. The sun was setting. The wagon with the shed was the one the hooded man had slipped into. It was leaving unnoticed, driven by the man who had, in truth, attacked Susanna. His clothes were different now. He had changed them in the small shed while the fight was getting underway. He changed his boots and placed the stained pair in a crevice under the wagon's back board. It was three days later that he found out that one of the boots had fallen onto the road as he was driving out of town—the left one, the one with the three-fingered stain.

A girl with bright eyes and long red hair lived with her family just the other side of the southern gates of the castle. Her name was Naomi; she was 12 years old. Naomi possessed an alert and attentive mind. She stood for over an hour after the fight to watch the people leave on this strange day. She saw the two women serve the big man as they moved him carefully and quickly to a nearby house. The man with the broken leg was carried off by two men.

Naomi had observed the details of the day from a distance. Then she heard the wheels of a wagon coming. The man driving did not see her; he never looked up. The wagon passed by and bumped over a small ridge in the road. Naomi turned at the sound of a muffled clunk. There was a boot in the road; it must have fallen off the wagon. Naomi looked toward the driver. He had not heard it fall. She walked over to look at the boot. She picked it up, but the wagon was gone. The boot had a yellowish/white three-fingered stain on it. For some reason, she wanted to keep it, so she did.

# Chapter Nine

# VALLEY OF SHAME

Mark survived by the grace of God, the faith-filled prayers of his family and the tender compassions of his wife and mother. But it took six months of care to regain most of his strength. The medicinal plant his mother used to treat the wound prevented a deep infection from developing. But, had the knife simply been 1/4-inch longer, he would not be alive. That is, if you call the shame he was overwhelmed with living.

As tough as the road of physical recovery was, the shame of his public display and the carnal ferocity of his behavior were much harder to endure. In addition to all that, the anger he freely exploded with had created an inner weakness, which made him unable to serve Susanna as she went through the agony of her disfigurement. And so, a terrible gap was growing between him and the most significant person in his world.

James was disappointed. Elizabeth spoke not a word, but Mark knew he had broken her heart, too. The greatest shame was his failure to honor the Lord. He had given himself permission to act in an ungodly way, contrary to the Word of God, his family's priorities, and the king's training. He was immediately placed on restricted status with the Royal Blue Guard until he was healthy. Then he would need to appear before the king for a decision on his conduct. He was in an utterly humiliated state.

Mark had almost always walked in and received honor. Such had been his path from childhood. The shame coupled with the fact that he had so readily expressed his arrogant pursuit of vengeance in public before young and old was devastating.

Mark was bedridden for weeks, experiencing pain and weakness he never knew existed. The wound was deep and the damage it caused was even worse than he had imagined. Wounds to the core of the body attack the seat of our strength. Those wounds are the hardest and longest to recover from.

He had known better than to act that way. The king had chosen him for many royal assignments, and more than that, had entrusted him with high privileges as a member of the Blue Guard. He had been given the title, the 'king's friend.' Mark had terribly shamed that. He had trespassed, at egregious levels, all the stations of honor in his life. The Longstreet name, the king's name, and his own name were diminished. He had also sunk a 'sword of sorrow' into his bride's heart. She was the clearest example of purity and holiness he had known. And now, she had to forsake her own pain to serve him with a scarred face.

She said nothing to him of her profound grief, which made it even worse. The burden was unbearable. But he could not deal with it as he needed to because he was too weak. He had great need to go to his prayer place and cry out to the Lord. But the strength to do so was not there. The crying hurt him physically, and twice he reopened the wound. He must wait and let the shame simmer inside. He found himself in an agony beyond description. Mark would later describe it in this way:

"This is the lowest point of my life. I have betrayed the best people in my world. I threw away the principles of God's Word, and completely disregarded the code and honor of my king. Here I am the king's friend, and I am acting like a pagan. Above all, I rebelled against the covenant of my God. I trespassed it without hesitation. These are but a few of the sins I so readily and gladly gave myself the freedom to commit.

"The first few days, I was more unconscious than awake, yet my heart was in constant turmoil. The appalling evil of my dreams was horrific. My mind was a whirlpool of anxiety, accusations, and fear. Visions of blood and violence were flung about in my thoughts like leaves in a storm. The swirl of memories came unsolicited. Much later, Susanna told me I had groaned and winced and wrestled constantly during the first days. That first week, she felt she would lose me every night.

"If the knife Erik threw had been just a bit longer, I would be dead. Honestly, there have been days, I wished I were. When I finally woke up and began to drink water and take some soup, hope was gained that I could recuperate physically. But that was also the beginning of a very deep and dark night for my soul. I felt as though I was choking, suffocating, and life was simply draining out of me. The burden of my sin was unbearable. There seemed not even the smallest part of the Lord in or near me, at least not that I could sense. I was enveloped in a deep darkness that I had created.

"I did not know how to overcome it. The shame was a mountain piled on top of me. The images of my rage played out like a living picture in my mind's eye over and over. I did not try to remember. These ugly memories came without my permission and in vivid detail. I had no control over any of it. Over and over, I would be in the fight with Erik again. I saw every swing of my sword and his knife. I heard each sound of the blades clashing and felt in my body the pains of the cutting. Worst of all, I was feeling again, my enjoyment of the rage. I craved the vengeance and enjoyed it as I remembered. I was undone at the evil in me. The feelings increased each time the memories came … and each time … I was more condemned.

"Previously, I had thought the picture of seeing Wayne fall off the rock was terrible and would never leave me, but these stark memories grew more powerful each time they came. I could not explain them to anyone. I saw myself as barbaric and beast-like. There were no other words to describe it. I was convinced I was evil. I was certain I was losing my mind. No one could understand the weight of these recollections. I was reliving the event in the same intensity I had when it happened. I was being haunted by the cruelties I had inflicted.

"The swirling images came as a tornado of terror: Susanna's bleeding face … Erik's knife slashing … the pain of Erik cutting my arms … the groans of the crowd … Susanna's bleeding face … the man running with the stain on his boot … seeing the stain up close on his boot at Erik's feet. I couldn't help but wonder why I remembered that stain so often and so precisely. Over and over my mind tracked the memory: Susanna's bloody face again … the shock of being pierced by the knife without seeing it thrown … the boiling rage in me … the gladness I felt when I hurt him … Susanna's face after she walked up to me. She was bandaged and bloody and deeply distressed for me. The image of her saddened face remains embossed in my memory to this day.

"I had acted like an ungodly animal, completely unrestrained. I conducted myself as an evil fool. I had done what Erik wanted. He was willing to kill me, but to humiliate me was better as far as he was concerned, and I had played into his scheme. I had sinned against the Lord, my oath to the king, the honor of my family name, my bride and on top of that, my children had seen the uncontrolled violence of their father. All of it was a burden beyond description.

"As the slow recovery began and I took short walks, I realized the town was ashamed of me as well. The eyes cast my way, the whispers as I hobbled by. The strength of the Lord's blessing everyone had talked about before the fight had lessened. Since that day, that blessing was restrained. I felt I had helped open a door for evil forces to come back. Here I am, a warrior for the king, and I opened a portal for evil forces to enter.

"After 15 weeks, I was still weak, but I was able to appear before the king. It was a terrible day. I feared the appointment to come before him. He was clearly displeased. I said not one word. After I entered and bowed, he spoke, 'Sir, Mark, your deeds as they have been reported to me and verified by many witnesses, have brought reproach to the realm as you dishonored your oath to the kingdom and your brothers in the Blue Guard. By your actions, you have refuted the honor of your family name, your wife's honor and shamed the authority entrusted to you. And the greatest reproach is the fact that you shamed the Lord and the oath you pledged to His kingdom. You and your wife will spend the next 40 days in prayer and then tell me what you know. I will make the decision about your future and your sentence at that time. You are dismissed.'"

"As I exited the throne room, backing out from the king's face, I found his words to be strange and painful. How could I address this additional delay without knowing what would happen to me as his discipline? The king's chamberlain told me of a cabin several miles away. The king had arranged for Susanna and me to stay there during the 40 days of prayer. Those days were to begin immediately. I wondered why the king required Susanna to go. I guessed it was to continue to serve as my nurse. Little did I realize the king's wisdom extended far beyond my physical needs for care."

Mark and Susanna made the journey to the prayer cabin early the next morning. They had always enjoyed open conversations … not now. Silence reigned. The ride in the king's wagon took four hours. They had to stop three times and allow the wound to rest from the constant jostling of the wagon wheels. The bumpy road antagonized the still-reddened scarred section of his abdomen. Even when they stopped, they did not speak. Those four hours felt like a month. Every time Mark thought of some way to begin, the words were throttled in his throat and never formed. So, they traveled wordless.

At last, they came to the small log structure near a smooth flowing stream with tree-lined pathways. The cabin was nestled in a beautiful setting with an oaken patio on the back. It was decked with benches that faced the stream. Mark slowly unpacked the wagon and Susanna began to prepare lunch … in silence.

Mark found himself overwhelmed with a paralyzed heart. There was no starting place; no topic to begin with. He turned from Susanna and stood outside waiting … for what … he did not know.

The cabin had been cleaned and was framed around a large open space. A suspended curtain defined the bedroom. Servants would bring supplies every few days from the king. These supplies were provided wordlessly. The provision was more than enough, and the strength of the king's heart toward them in this crisis also worked in Mark a greater degree of understanding in how much he had dishonored him. The king's goodness was like a sword directed toward Mark's selfish raging, and it was cutting into his heart and leading him to repent.

After a few moments outside, Mark knew he must make some effort. He turned and stepped slowly into the cabin. He walked over to her. Gently and with no words, he placed his hand on the back of hers to stop her activity. She did not resist. She had been waiting on him.

Mark tenderly gripped her hand and led her to the back patio. Picking up two cushions, they made the way to the patio door. She sat on the cushions he positioned on the bench. Mark stood for a moment, then sat and wondered how to begin. What could he do? What could he say?

He sighed again, and then, without warning, tears exploded from deep within his body as he uncontrollably convulsed with the shame. A flood of grief and pain swept over Mark as he groaned and cried with no idea where this river of sorrow would transport him. The scar was throbbing, but he did not care about that anymore. He desperately needed to get right before his God and his wife.

> He desperately needed to get right before his God and his wife.

Susanna sat there, listening to his groaning sobs, and witnessing the heaving of his body. The roaring agony of his rebellion against the Lord's ways came out in torrents of grief as his mountainous shame flooded up and out. At one point, Mark's bones were trembling. He would never be able to find the words to explain what seemed to be a strong force grabbing his ankles with huge hands at the bones, and it shook him from the ankles up and the bones out.

Marks' eyes emptied buckets of tears. His body released the poison of his deeds in trembling deep weeping. Susanna sat silently and motionless. The Lord was working in him. She could do nothing but observe.

It was terrible … ugly … and utterly holy. The heavenly clean One was working in the depths of the unclean one. The one true King dealt with Mark's perverse, stubborn, and hidden weaknesses. His holy hammer drove out the secret carnal justifications for his anger.

"I remember I could do nothing but cry for two hours. Words would begin to form from my heart. But each time, they were hushed by the deep heaving from my soul's roots. Finally, in broken sentences and weak tones, I scratched out, 'Lord of all, You alone are right, and You made me … I have sinned … against You ... Your ways … Your Word.'"

And, for two more hours Mark confessed to his God and before his bride, the sins of his anger and rage and foolishness. Including his idolatrous lust for vengeance against Erik, he confessed the arrogance and evil permission he had given himself to work out such violence. He was repulsed to see the reality of his capacity to do evil. He knew Susanna was praying, but she said nothing. She knew it is not wise to interrupt someone who is cleansing their soul before God. She knew Mark had much to unload. The human tendency to make someone feel better in such times of repentance prevents the Lord from purging us at the deepest of necessary levels.

> The human tendency to make someone feel better in such times of repentance prevents the Lord from purging us at the deepest of necessary levels.

Finally, the tears stopped. Mark was exhausted. Susanna was quiet. They ate a late, small supper. They had missed lunch and spoke only the words needed to conduct the meal. She was not resisting Mark. She did understand the need to allow the brokenness to remain and root into him. Mark was certain his repentance was not finished. But a small root of life had been placed inside, and it could deepen from there.

They both knew he must at least begin his repentance toward her. The sun had already set, but this type of action could not be determined by the timelines of human reasoning. People are often guilty of expecting the Lord to cater to their likings and preferences, but that can never be the attitude of an agent of the king. Trying to fit repentance into a planned timeframe is like trying to schedule the birth of a baby. No one schedules repentance with God. People can only respond to Him when He draws them. The inconvenience of it is essential, so that even the timing is determined by Him.

Slowly, with halting phrases, Mark asked, "What did I make you feel like when you saw how I acted?"

For the first time in more than three months, Susanna looked at him as the woman who knew him. The scar on her forehead was healing and looked less inflamed, but they both knew it would never be removed. Mark felt the scar his actions produced inside her that day were much worse and would never be removed either. She could lay her hair across most of it, but one end of the scar or the other remained visible no matter what she did with her hair.

Mark was yearning to hear from her. His heart was open— no matter what she said. He wanted to hear her. He needed to hear her. He dreaded hearing her.

Susanna had always been a light of God's life: holy, free, and wise. As she began to share the words that had been forming in her for weeks, she spoke them accurately, and with her eyes fixed on his. She had been hurt by Mark in the lowest reaches of her trust—a breach only a miracle from the Lord could fill.

He was remembering the secrets of the swords his family made. Much like the forming of a sword, the weakened parts of his heart had to be hammered out, and then sanctified in the fire of the Lord's forgiveness, so he would never forget his sins had been forgiven. Such was the unique tenderness God expressed toward Mark's most unlovely ways.

Susanna spoke until midnight as Mark cried more from the dearest part of his heart. She was not trying to cause him further pain. She was processing the repentance and speaking the truth in a love that was not merely human. All these things occurred on the first day. There were 39 days to go.

At 1:00 in the morning, Susanna told Mark with a completely genuine heart that she forgave him and loved him. Then she hesitated, and said, "But I do not trust you ... I love you, but I do not trust you."

Those words went deeper than Erik's knife had.

As the remaining days progressed, Mark knew he had to regain her trust. Trust is not automatic. Love is strong, but trust is fragile. Trust can be regained, but it must be rebuilt by consistent actions **and** kindness. Mark confessed his wickedness to her as he had toward the Lord, and then slowly, they moved forward.

Susanna and Mark spent the next 39 days in the heat of the Lord's searching gaze. The experience was a reminder of the days Jesus spent being tempted in the desert. Or the days for Elijah in the wilderness after he fled from Jezebel.

The Bible says the Spirit searches the depths of God.

Mark realized that if the Holy Spirit does that with God, the Spirit could and would certainly search him. HE did. The Spirit, Who is Holy God uncovered selfish motives and sinful intentions Mark had never conceived could be in his heart. He was made aware of a religious arrogance and saw how his heart craved attention. He had always been able to say the right words, but his heart was far from wanting the Lord to be honored. His lust for vengeance had proved this. "At my base, I was arrogant and a hypocrite. I was not an amen-man."

Mark remembered a sermon from a monk who had spoken at the church meeting. The monk said, "The one thing any person can do to most dramatically change their life is to courageously face who they are without the Lord, and then they must courageously face who they are meant to be in the Lord. Both of those revelations require courage to see and only the Lord can reveal them to us."

> "The one thing any person can do to most dramatically change their life is to courageously face who they are without the Lord, and then they must courageously face who they are meant to be in the Lord."

Tears came repeatedly. Susanna began to cry with Mark. The Bible speaks of the fear of the Lord. But Mark had never known what that meant until those days were spent in front of Him. Mark stood in front of the Almighty God with no defense.

The Lord is right. He is always right. The greatest pressure that can be put on a human is the pressure of being in the presence of the Lord with no walls between. Isaiah saw the Lord and cried out, "Woe is me, for I am a man of unclean lips." Every time an angel was revealed in the Bible, the person seeing the angel was stricken with fear. Is it not reasonable that seeing the Lord Himself would be more fearsome?

> The greatest pressure that can be put on a human is the pressure of being in the presence of the Lord with no walls between.

136

John, Moses, Daniel, and Ezekiel each saw the Lord and fell on their faces like dead men. One verse says, "No one can see the Lord and live." Mark realized that was happening to him. God wanted Mark to see Him and die ... to his old ways. Mark was not seeing Him with human eyes, but with the eyes of his heart. But Mark was seeing the Lord ... it was fearful, and he was dying ... to his old ways. Mark had known he was a believer in the Lord before this. He knew he was His son, but the weeks set apart to do nothing but seek God were transforming Mark at a spiritually molecular depth. It was indescribable. He was not the same man.

One verse declares, "Our God is a consuming fire." Mark had put blades in the fire for years. If God was indeed making him into a sword, this was the baptism of fire that could form his unique curve. Waters of weeping pierced his deepest parts. Mark was in the furnace of God's face. His response was more repentance and more tears. In many ways, Mark was seeing Him for the first time. God was whispering to Mark, revealing His secrets, and Mark was smitten with the privilege.

And then, when they had been there 37 days, and the fire was the hottest, when he thought he could stand no more, Susanna and Mark began to sing to the Lord while in His fire. And Mark became, by the hand of God, a new man. One night they sang to Him with hearts unrestricted for two hours. Then they sat silently in front of Him for another two hours. The weight of His face was shining into their hearts. It changed them and melted them together as two irons into a new oneness. This was a holy encounter in His fire.

Susanna had been completely honest with him about the fight. She revealed her shame at his behavior and how she felt uncovered and unprotected because of his actions. Susanna's tears made Mark's heart hurt as he reckoned with the depth of the pain inflicted on the lady he loved. Mark had vowed to God to honor her and protect her; yet, he had done neither by his deeds. She told him the strength and honor of his heart had always been her real confidence in him whenever they had faced trouble.

While looking deeply into his eyes, she said, "Ultimately Mark, my stability and confidence was never in your physical abilities, but it was always your loyalty to Jesus that made me secure."

Her truthful corrections disarmed Mark of his carnal confidence in the strength of his body. With fearsome trembling, she revealed how she felt so ugly now, because of the scar and then confessed her shame at her vain concern about her appearance. They both wept before God and held each other for an hour of tears.

The 40 days were the darkest, deepest, and most powerful days they had ever known before God. He met them. He helped them both. He changed them.

The last evening, before returning to the king, Susanna and Mark experienced true holy matrimony. They spent the final hours praying and singing and looking to the Lord. He met them and settled them into Himself in ways that were fresh and new—ways they had never experienced.

For anyone who has never imagined doing this kind of

focused pursuing of the Lord, the seeking of His face and hearing His heart, all this may sound strange. But, once anyone has seen Him with the eyes of their heart, they will know they need Him, and this kind of pursuing of Him will not be strange at all.

> But, once anyone has seen Him with the eyes of their heart, they will know they need Him, and this kind of pursuing of Him will not be strange at all.

In the years ahead, Mark and Susanna would remember the weight of His presence and the wonder of His grace into their household. The intensity of that time with God became the rock of their home's foundation for the rest of their days. As fearsome and terrible as those days were, they often wished to be back in that cabin with their fiery God.

> As fearsome and terrible as those days were, they often wished to be back in that cabin with their fiery God.

On day 40, they prepared to go back to their home and the meeting with the king. Though there was uncertainty about the king's decision, the beginnings of joy were returning. Mark realized why the earthly king had sent them on this 40-day pursuit. King Egbert knew what the King of heaven could do with them, if they gave Him the time. Since then, Mark made it a practice to set aside days to go and meet alone with God every year. Sometimes, Susanna joined him. Each time, Mark found the experience life-giving.

Mark knew the king would put him under some type of

139

discipline. Perhaps it would be permanently dismissed from the Blue Guard. If the king decreed that, Mark would accept it as a just decision. By God's kindest of graces, Mark had been restored back to a right position in Him; that was the most important thing. He would go to the castle as soon as he had settled Susanna back at the house.

On the road home, they smiled for the first time in a long time. They laughed a little and spoke of the future, regardless of the king's decision. The strength of hope was rising. As they neared their house, a young girl was playing with friends on the lane. At their approach, she left the friends and drew near to them. "Hello, Sir Mark, my name is Naomi."

"Hello, Naomi, how are you?"

"I saw the fight you had at the festival months ago," she remarked quite openly.

Mark was not ready for this sudden public reference to sins so recently forgiven. But he replied softly, "Yes, I am that man."

With no delay, Naomi perked up, "I saw the mark on the boot of the man who was fighting you. I have his boot."

Mark's heart skipped a beat, "What did you say?"

"I have his boot. Stay here, I will get it." She turned and ran into her house while Susanna and Mark sat in wonderment. He could not grasp what Naomi said. *"What did she mean?"*

She came back with the boot and said, "It dropped off the wagon he was driving." Naomi told her story about picking it up. Mark stared carefully and slowly at the boot, turning it side to side in his strong hands. He placed Naomi's boot next to the boot in his memory. For some reason, that image of Erik's boot had been frozen in his mind's eye. He knew why now. The boot in his hand could not be the same boot he had seen on Erik's foot. There was a slight discrepancy in the third outside stain. Erik had both his boots on when he was carried off. This boot was obviously not Erik's boot.

Suddenly, it hit Mark as a hundred stones hurled at the same time. He had been so wrong. Erik was not the one who had cut Susanna! Just as the men had said, "Erik has been with us," was their clear statement and Mark had refused to believe them. Someone wanted Mark to think it was Erik, and whoever it was, they wanted Mark to hurt Erik by attacking Susanna. Somehow, that person knew the clothes Erik would wear, the hooded garment and the stained boot.

Mark fell over in the wagon and sobbed again. He would have to repent to Erik. Naomi was surprised by Mark's strong tears, but she waited patiently. When he finally regained his composure, he asked, "Naomi, may I take this boot?"

"Sure, I don't need it. It is too big for either one of my feet."

Grinning faintly at her remark, Mark said, "Thank you very much. Farewell."

Clearly, the stain on this boot had been smeared by three fingers. Obviously, the boot in Mark's hand was not the boot Erik had been wearing. Someone had tried to frame Erik and used Mark to carry out the vengeance. Mark felt he needed 40 more days of prayer. The self-confidence and the arrogance Mark had moved in struck him again with the need to repent. He was trembling with a fresh shame.

# Chapter Ten

# FULLER FORGIVENESS

James and Elizabeth had been calling out to the Lord every morning and every night for Susanna and Mark during their 40 days away. King Egbert had done the same. He was asking the Lord for wisdom on how to discipline Mark. He believed he heard from the Lord what to do, but the grace that could come to Mark depended on what he reported to the king when he returned.

Mark unloaded the wagon, after Susanna and he greeted the children. The reunion was packed with emotion. The old joy— no, it was a new joy that was coming into their home. It was like fresh air. It was a deeper joy that was beginning to be released in both. After greeting all the children and settling in, Mark set his heart and feet to go see King Egbert. He made his way with a soft heart. The time he had met the king after the first fight with the Vikings, he was humble, but he knew now, that this time was different. It would take no effort to be humble. He was genuinely humble at the root of his heart. He found it pleasantly satisfying not to be fighting internally for recognition. The fresh breeze of deep humility wafted through his soul.

The king's countenance was stern as Mark entered. Mark walked in, bowed, and continued the motion until he was on his knees … and waited.

"Sir Mark, give the report of your time away. You can be sure I will verify with your spouse all you report. It would be wise for you to speak fully to me with nothing unsaid ... no shadows. This requirement of complete honesty comes from God's dealings with me. Now, what do you say?"

Mark remained on his knees. The story was revealed cleanly from Mark's heart. He took his time, not to take advantage of the king, but to solidify the account into the king's ears. Mark sensed no impatience on the king's part. He included details of how the Lord had dealt with him, and how he had cried out, and how Susanna was there for the whole thing.

He even spoke of things he and Susanna had shared. No detail should be hidden from the king in a circumstance like this. Mark spoke for more than an hour, often with tears, as he relived those profound days in front of his God. He ended by expressing genuine gratitude for the king's wise and just decision to send them away together.

King Egbert sat in silence. He was a wise elder in the ways of the Lord. He was not impulsively impressed by dramatic displays. His eyes and heart had journeyed through complex relations for over 30 years, and part of the wisdom he had gained included just how much strength to exert in a specific moment. The king listened deeply. He was looking for the substance of deep repentance, much more than an emotional catharsis. As Mark spoke, the king heard what he needed to hear.

"Sir Mark, stand to your feet!" The king stared into Mark's countenance as if assessing him on the inside. He began to speak slowly. "My father sent me to that cabin for 40 days the year before I was made king. I can smell the fragrance of the Lord on you and your words. I have felt the hammer of the Lord pounding out the impurities of my own soul. There is no way for us to see ourselves clearly without the Spirit of God showing who we are in the depths of our selfish complexities. It is so easy for us to justify generational carnalities as if they are approved by God because they have been in our family for so long. I accept your report."

Mark eased inside—well, not too much. He was confident the king's decision would be the Lord's decision.

"You shall serve for two weeks at a time in the following six places. First you are assigned to the Royal stable, then the kitchen, the pig lot, the garden, the bath house for the soldiers, and finally, the training of the new recruits. In addition, you will teach the children's class at the monastery every Sunday morning during this discipline. It may be your heart will soften further by serving the children. You will report for each of these assignments every morning before sunrise and work until dusk. When you have completed these six places of service, we will see what else the Lord requires."

"Yes, your Majesty. Thank you. Your Majesty, if I may, could I submit one more matter to you?"

"You may."

Mark slowly and quietly shared the story about the boot found by the girl, Naomi. He told the king of his clear image of the three-fingered stain, and the difference between what he had seen on Erik's boot and what he saw on the boot from Naomi. The point was, how could Naomi have Erik's boot? Erik was carried off with his broken leg and both boots were on his feet. Then, with fresh tears, Mark pulled the stained boot from his bag. He had been wrong. Erik was being framed. Perhaps it had been a previous foe he had hurt before he was transformed.

Mark was clear Erik was not the one who had attacked Susanna, and he promised King Egbert he would search for Erik and repent to him fully. Mark cried more godly tears as he left the king's chamber.

When Mark arrived home, James and Elizabeth were there. The evening was a holy family time as Mark confessed the sins he had committed, with strong and genuine grief before his parents and the children. He finished by asking everyone to please forgive him, and Jennifer ran up to embrace him saying loudly, "Daddy, I 'give' you, I 'give' you."

He cried new tears of love at her faith and grace. He realized children do not require parents to be perfect, but they do expect honesty and a willingness to acknowledge wrongs and ask for forgiveness. Instead of losing respect with his children, they respected him more for his open heart about his sin.

After the children were sent to bed, James and Elizabeth spent a brief time of intense communication with them. Again, the words were sacred and mature. The tears on all sides were full and sincere. Then, James and Elizabeth left for the castle. James had stopped working in the forge a few months ago. Now, he was training the other men and soldiers in smithy skills and swordsmanship. He had become known as the gray-haired senior with wise hands and a wiser heart. Instead of creating and sharpening weapons, he was now sharpening the 'heart-edges' of the men in the king's service.

Mark spent the 12 weeks of his discipline in the six areas of service and received outstanding grades from all the supervisor's reports to the king. He found the time in the pig lot was especially disgusting, but he gained a much greater appreciation for those who do the necessary, but often unrecognized work. He vowed to give ready honor to all who labored faithfully, whether recognized or not.

He would later remark the time teaching the children was his most treasured assignment. Truly, he had not taught them, instead, he was their student. The king released him to go back into training for the Blue Guard as a private. He would gain his former rank of captain when he passed all the tests of that level. Mark did it in record time. The scar on his abdomen had healed physically, but the stain of his sin was still open and near, reminding him of his weakness every day.

Mark worked daily in the assignments the king had ordered. He sought the Lord, and each day he walked and worked with and listened to Susanna. He would ask anyone in the community that he could about Erik and how to get in touch with him. Though Mark could not locate him, he continued searching for Erik.

There was another challenge to Mark's repentance being fully expressed. He was beginning to regain some of the respect he lost with the people of the community. His humility was recognized as authentic, and the former honor was slowly being restored because he had so honestly faced his shameful deeds. For weeks, as he moved through the discipline by the king, Mark would often start a conversation by asking, "Would you allow me to apologize to you for my wrongful actions?"

People were touched by his brokenness. Others began to face their own shameful ways at deeper places since Mark was supplying an excellent expression of it. The blessings of the previous 'open heaven' were slipping back into town.

An older man was traveling through the area of the king's castle. He was headed further south to live out his final days on his children's farm. His grandson was making the trip with him. All his earthly goods were in a wagon. He had intended to stop at the castle to see it, since he had never been there before. On that day, James and Elizabeth happened to be in the castle plaza. When the three of them saw each other, all three erupted in glad smiles and embraced each other with strong heartfelt care. They had been friends for years in Monkwearmout and had not seen each other since the move to the castle. They knew immediately there would be a schedule change for lunch.

"We are not going to have a dear friend come by and then go on our way. Godly friendships are among the greatest gifts God gives. You must eat with us today. It is so good to see you and your grandson!"

The decision was made. After the midday meal, as expected, the stories began. Laughter erupted frequently over the stories they all knew. And delight was shared both ways at the new stories generated since the last time they had seen each other. Then offhandedly, while reminiscing about the port and the forge. The man said, "Do you remember when that box of dirt you brought from the Japanese guy was stolen from your wagon at the monastery?"

James and Elizabeth both said, "Of course we do."

"Well, we found out who stole it."

"Really, who was it?"

"A group of young men did it. But one of them had a change of heart about the theft and told his parents last month about doing it. He was mixed in with a mean man who is an expert with a knife. He was the leader of that bunch. We heard he had a rough time growing up. His mom died in a fire when he was young, and …"

James interrupted, "He was 8-years-old when his mom died, right? And his name is Erik?"

"Why yes, that is right. How did you know that?"

"We know him; that is all we need to say."

The evening with the old friend continued, but James and Elizabeth were stuck inside with the revelation of who the thief was and his current connection with Mark. The old friend and his grandson left just before dinner.

James and Elizabeth told Mark and the family the next morning. For Mark, it was another knife to his gut by Erik. Here he was seeking him out to ask for forgiveness, and now, the extra load of the theft was also revealed. Mark was humbled enough to respond rightly. He went to a private place that afternoon and prayed. All he could consider were verses from the Bible about forgiving those who sin against us. He remembered his own sin and how gracious the Lord had been with him, then the words of Jesus, "Freely you have received, freely give."

Mark had freely received from the Lord the grace and

forgiveness when he did not deserve it. With that very grace, he would give that same forgiveness out to someone who did not deserve it. This was especially true since Erik had been transformed. Mark knew he must release this old trespass. He did. Now, he must find Erik and repent to him face to face. Mark was being changed at molecular levels by the hammer of God's love in the forge of day-to-day relationships. He was becoming an amen-man.

# Chapter Eleven

## THE TRUTH!
(What really happened **"before"** the 2nd fight.)

Before the second fight began, Erik had been presenting himself as one who had been changed by the Lord, but the truth was he had not changed at all. Instead, he had matured his anger into a perversely evil scheme. Erik was not at peace. He had changed, but not for the better. He was on fire and riveted into revenge. After the first fight, when Mark broke Erik's wrist and cut his face, Erik became fueled by a death-wish against Mark. He had stolen Erik's knife; it was the only thing he cherished. In addition, the cut on his chin of his heretofore unscarred face, was the greatest wound. Now, he was boiling with hatred. He was focused. Erik was exhilarated! He had a reason to live that made him glad. All his abilities were channeled into hurting the girl and killing the man.

He worked and exercised his wrist until it was much stronger than before. Hours and hours of training again and again, learning new skills and making them perfect. He had learned to throw the knife with both hands, and from now on, he would carry three knives. The first was larger and better than the knife Mark had taken. The other two were smaller with one hidden in a sheath at his back and the third inside the top lip of his boot. These two extra knives were part of Erik's growing scheme to kill Mark.

He knew it was one thing to train and prepare to fight Mark, but since Mark was in the king's Royal Blue Guard, it would be quite another to be justified in doing so. Erik's plan must be without flaw. There must be no charge against Erik after he hurt Susanna and killed Mark. But how? He must create some context to force Mark to initiate an attack against him. That way, Erik would not be guilty of murder. He would be defending himself.

His twisted heart housed a cruel delight in injustice. Demons assisted him. The same kind of demons which had filled the Berserkers, were thrilled to fill Erik's mind and body with their insane chaos. Erik was willing to receive the help. He liked the evil. The idea that would protect him from a murder charge came to him like a fiery dart from outside his own thinking and entered his dark heart. The picture for the plan formed in his understanding, in splendidly violent detail.

He called together his five disciple-partners and lined out all the steps. The tasks were made to each one, and the specifics were refined over several months. Erik grinned from the depth of his evil heart over the excellent scheme. He would set it up in the same marketplace where Mark had cut his chin, but this time the cutting would be on Mark and his bride. The plan would be carried out on the last day of the fall festival after the harvest had been taken in. There would be a large crowd. That would be … perfect!

These five were cut from the same historic cloth as Erik. All of them had been hardened by the harsh treatment received from their parents. They were mean and they honored the severity of the hatred growing in Erik. The five were fortified by the fire in him. They were thrilled with his rage. The five were younger than Erik, but two of them were stronger and larger than him. He practiced his fighting style against Mark with the two larger men, since they were closer to Mark's size. He would wrap their arms and body with cloth and leather to avoid cutting them. He also wrapped their necks with leather collars because he had a new move as his planned final blow for Mark.

Men of this nature always produce great harm. Erik would be successful at doing that. He planned and trained day and night. He did not go to the castle market for over a year and a half. He was immersed in his anger. He waited until the iniquity in him had found its full curve of violence. A perverse joy boiled in Erik, feeding itself and gaining the revengeful momentum of reckless payback, refined by an evil energy.

Erik had to be right to attack Mark. He had to be justified in fighting him. The five began to implement the details of the plan. The first step of the plan meant Erik had to take a walk. He went six miles down the lane to speak with the Smithson family. He walked up to the house, and with a pleasant voice greeted Mr. Smithson: "Hello Sir," and Erik began a friendly conversation. In a few minutes, he offered to help with some of the farm work. Mr. Smithson was shocked, but hesitantly allowed him to help. For two hours, Erik worked as hard as any man Mr. Smithson had ever seen. When Erik left, Smithson was stunned, *"Who was that man?"*

For several months, Erik came twice a week and worked

153

like a horse, serving in any way he could. He never complained and never explained why he was helping. One time, while eating a meal with the Smithson family, Erik seemed to open his heart. Erik admitted he was trying to make up for some bad stuff he had done, but then his voice trailed off. Apart from that conversation, it could be said that Erik was delightful.

Mr. Smithson found himself trusting Erik, grateful for his glad service. He attributed his kind behavior to the blessing from heaven being spoken of around the castle. For whatever reason, Mr. Smithson was thankful.

His wife and only son had died in a freak accident with a bull two years previously. The grief had rooted into him and his 24-year-old daughter, NanLee. The unusual name was formed by combining those of her two grandmothers. She was very pretty. Her blue eyes were deep pools, and her light brown hair was long over her shoulders. Her winsome personality made her enjoyable to be around. Her smile was genuine. Her laugh was infectious and free. You can at times discern the depth of liberty in a heart by how freely and genuinely they laugh. She had a generous heart and was strong in a feminine way. She was the kind of lady whose beauty emerged and increased from the inside.

(Elizabeth had spoken of women who look lovely on the outside, but inside, they were not pretty. Those ladies had to rely on their beautiful exterior, but if they had no true inner loveliness, the years never treated them well. They became unattractive physically as they aged. "The truth is," she said, "beauty is real when it comes from the inside. Outside beauty will fade if the inside is ugly. But, inside beauty will always win. You want to marry a lady with beauty on the inside. She becomes more attractive the longer she lives.") NanLee was that kind of beautiful lady inside and out.

Erik was positioning a particularly devious part of his scheme by working for Mr. Smithson, yet his energy was still directed against Mark. Erik had never been truly for anyone except himself. His plan was working.

However, there was one problem—it was a growing problem. His fake service was attracting NanLee's attention. Erik could tell she was treating him more openly, which bothered him. He didn't want her attention. He hated it … *or did he?* The questioning inside made him angry. This would only be going on for a few more months, and then he would be rid of her. But she was becoming a distraction to his focus, and he found himself unwittingly expecting and anticipating seeing her whenever he approached their farm.

The five were working with other farmers to arrange for the use of two wagons to help carry their harvest abundance to the festival. Each detail was part of the plan. They needed wood to build a portable shed-like structure to carry on the wagon. They purchased several kinds of cloth, and then asked two different ladies, who did not know one another to make exact replicas of the same pants, shirt, overshirt and a crimson colored robe with a hood. He purchased two pairs of the same kind of boots. The robe with the hood was the most important part of each set of clothes. The two sets of clothes had to match exactly. One set of clothes would fit Erik perfectly. The other would fit one of the five, who was the same size as Erik. Both sets matched perfectly.

The five worked and trained alongside Erik. They honed their story, rehearsing it over and over. They considered fine details and tried to imagine mistakes and how to overcome them. They worked the neighbors, selling them the characters they wanted to portray. Erik worked harder than all of them. His revenge was maturing and anxious to be expressed. He rested each night practicing his moves in his mind. He was ready. The fall festival was set for the next weekend, and the detailed steps of the scheme were not finalized and had been refined to the second. The five and Erik were ready for their wrongness to go exactly as they anticipated.

Erik must make one last visit to the Smithson farm before he and the five made the trip to the castle marketplace with the wagons. But this growing, uneasy pleasure had seeded into his heart. NanLee had been planting it in him over the months he had been serving her dad. She liked him. Erik knew it, and a twinge of guilt was forming inside. Although small and easy to push aside, the guilt rose unsolicited each time he went to the farm. He was glad this was the last time he would go to the Smithson home. Maybe she would not be there. Anyway, he planned to move south after this deed was done.

As Erik drew near, he smiled on the outside, but inside he groaned. NanLee was at the gate waiting. To Erik, she was growing lovelier each time. He did enjoy her, but her care for him was getting in the way. He didn't want to like her. He wanted to kill Mark. He needed to be able to remain focused on his task.

"Hello," Erik said, with a double-hearted smile. NanLee broke into a sincere smile, opened the gate and moved easily toward him. He had never had any girl really like him. He was always self-conscious about the scar on his chin. NanLee ignored it. Erik wondered why. He was nervous and didn't want to deceive her, but he was deceiving her. And now an anger rose in him—against himself. The conflict was terrible. His focus was breaking. He needed to get out of there. However, he had this part of him that wanted to stay with her.

"It is always so good to see you, Erik." Her words broke into his thoughts. She spoke his name with a genuine affection. There was no malice, no anger, no fear in her toward him. She liked him. Erik knew that because it was the first time anyone had ever really liked him. Her kindness was like cold water on a hot day. Her smile was so inviting. He wanted to stay—and that made him even angrier with himself.

"Uh, where is your dad?" mustered Erik, in an awkward effort to redirect the conversation. His heart still wanted more of her kind words. He found a place forming inside that wanted to protect her. *"What was that?"* he questioned himself. He did not want to use her or take advantage. For the first time in his life, he was caring for someone else.

"He is working an errand on the far side of the farm," said NanLee. "He told me where the things are you will need for the trip to the marketplace this weekend. Are you still leaving for the festival next Monday?"

Erik stalled inside, distracted by her, caught himself staring.

157

"Well, are you?"

"Oh, uh, yes, we leave next Monday," he stammered. "Uh, where are the things we need for the wagon?"

"Come this way. They are next to those barrels by the barn door. Father put them there for you. My father is so grateful for your help. He has been discouraged since we lost mom and my brother." NanLee paused considering the loss. Erik was speechless in the stillness. He had no wisdom for pain. Then NanLee regathered her thoughts and said, "but since you came, it is like fresh air has come to him. He enjoys having a real man around."

*"She called me a real man."* No one had said anything nice about him—ever. He didn't like how much he found himself craving her care. They walked around the corner of the barn toward the barrels. NanLee was looking at Erik, and unexpectedly, she slipped and tripped over the root of a large tree. Suddenly, unintentionally she was falling across his body. Erik, without thinking, caught her easily with his left arm. Later, he would remember the way she fell and how it felt to catch her, to hold her up. He never forgot the way she relaxed into his strength.

Immediately as she fell, and while still cradled in his left arm, an adder, the only poisonous snake in Saxon lands, lay hidden between the barrels. Suddenly it stirred and coiled to strike. NanLee saw it. Erik moved with lightning-like reflexes. While still holding her, the new knife appeared in his right hand—a shiny, sharp blade flashing with a speed few could match. He nailed the head of the adder to the ground. In an instant—it was dead. NanLee, still at ease in his strength and still resting in his grasp, slowly regained her stance. As they backed away from the dead snake, she embraced him warmly and spoke with deep gratitude and said, "Thank you, Erik; you saved my life. I will never forget it." Then she placed a gentle kiss on his cheek.

*"She is not trying to get away from my embrace. Why is she willing for me to hold her? Why did she kiss me? I like how that felt. This is getting out of control!"*

He had been planning on killing a man and hurting his wife for almost two years, but now here he was saving the life of a beautiful lady. He stopped again and realized that NanLee had a way of consistently stopping his insides. But he thought it. *"She was beautiful. She is beautiful."* For the first time he allowed himself to enjoy the fact that she liked him, and he liked her. He was not fighting those feelings.

"You ... uh ... are nice to say those things. Uh ... well ... thanks for the things for the wagon. Uh ... bye, Nan."

Erik walked off wondering, *"Why did I call her Nan?"* He had never used her name before, much less given her a nickname.

As he strolled off, she called out, "I will see you at the market, 'snake-killer.'" NanLee was thrilled that he called her Nan! *"He has never called me by name before; I like Nan."* She smiled deeply as she watched him walk away.

Erik was crazy inside, and he grinned at the snake-killer title. *"Nan—sweet name. I like it, and he could still feel the touch of her lips on his cheek."* The kindness and care from a good lady created a storm in him. Despite her deepening influence, the conflict rose again. He had planned his vengeance against Mark for too long to change it now. So, by the time he reached his farm, he had fanned the flame of his revenge back into a blaze and Nan's tender words were locked up in a box at the back of his heart with a heavy lid on it. His anger was more comfortable than the care Nan had given him.

To put even more weight on that lid, Erik spent four hours in unrestrained fury as he practiced how he would kill Mark. By midnight, he was completely immersed in the heat of his hatred and Nan's kind words were not merely a distant memory—they had been buried.

The five and Erik were headed to the castle. They traveled the road with little conversation. As they neared the intersection to split off to the houses they would be staying in, they discussed in detail the plan to be executed two days later.

Just before they were to split up, Erik asked, "Where are the boots you will wear for our plan? I have an idea."

The man was surprised, but lifted them out of a woolen bag, "Here they are."

Erik took some bright yellowish/white mold from under a piece of tree bark and swiped a three-fingered stain on the outer left side of the left boot. Erik spoke forcefully, "Be sure you do not wipe that off. Do you understand? Do not wipe that off!"

The man nodded submissively, but with no understanding as to why the stain was so important.

Erik stayed with the wagon when the five dispersed. They would not speak to each other again until they came together three miles on the other side of the castle when the festival was over. Erik spent the next two days meeting people and smiling. He did not see Mark and did not want Mark to see him, at least not yet. People were talking about Erik as if something had changed with him. On the last day, some of the towns' people approached him and even initiated conversations. They all found themselves enjoying his company. The old man who knew his father said, "I have not seen Erik like this. He must have changed. Indeed, the Lord is visiting us if men like Erik can change."

Erik heard the words and was satisfied the trap was ready. The third day was the final day of the celebration. The crowd was filling up the plaza with conversations and good-natured fellowship. The market was peppered with scores of carts, tables and wagons displaying the bounty of the harvest. Erik glimpsed Mark and Susanna from a distance and hid behind a stall as they passed from view. The time was not yet.

The closing event for the last day of the festival was a crowd favorite. As in years before, the women played a game called hide and race in a large grass field near the forested grounds on the side of the castle. All the women would line up facing the castle, with their backs to the field. One lady would cross the 100-yard-long field and go and hide inside the tree line of the forest. The others would turn at the signal and try to find the one hiding. If, and when someone saw the lady hiding, she and the other ladies would race back to the starting line. The last lady there would be the one to hide the next time. Susanna had won that race, when Erik tried to kiss her. Erik knew she would be the first to hide.

This was the beginning of the sequence of pain he had devised. The man from the five, who looked like Erik and dressed exactly as Erik was, including the stained left boot, was already hiding in the forest before the game started. The real Erik was in the marketplace, over 100 yards away speaking with some men among the carts and wagons. He had smeared an exactly matching three-fingered stain of the same mold on his left boot.

He kept talking to the men he had befriended during the festival's last two days. He would stay there to talk and listen and wait. Only 5 minutes remained before the ladies' game started. He stayed where he was. He knew Mark would come to the last game. He would be ready for him when it was time to kill him. Erik was standing and talking with these men next to a wagon with its table and the small portable shed at the rear of it.

Now, the truth about Erik's motives in his devious plan could be recognized for what they were from the start. He had not changed—he didn't want to change. All he really wanted to do was engineer a scheme to hurt Susanna and kill Mark.

# Chapter Twelve

# ERIK'S TORTURED JOURNEY

Erik's plan did not work as he intended. His injuries were severe.

When Mark broke Erik's leg he was taken from the plaza and passed out. He was jolted awake by the pain and screamed as he writhed. He was exhausted and in a shocked agony. He could not keep still. Every move hurt, even lying still hurt. The only good thing, which was troublesome at the same time, was that Nan was holding his hand when he woke up. She really did care. He was in the greatest conflict of his life. Nan had no idea of his motives and the fight was his own vindictive scheme against Mark and Susanna. She had no clue that his service to their family was a ploy to deceive and advance his revenge. She still believed he was sincere about his changes. Erik was tortured inside and out.

Though Mark and Erik were both wrong in their actions, Erik was launched into his recovery-process from a completely different foundation than the one Mark had.

He was not ashamed of what he had done, except when he remembered Nan. He was glad about what he had done. He heard over the next few days that Mark had survived, but he reveled in the public humiliation Mark had received. Erik's leg was ugly, mangled, and now there were several more scars on his body in addition to the one on his chin. All of them had come at the hands of Mark! That agony was unbearable.

A man who knew how to care for warriors' wounds had been present the day of the fight. He saw and heard the leg snap at the knee. He examined it and discovered none of the bones had been broken, because the leg had disjointed exactly at the kneecap.

Erik went to sleep with great difficulty the first night and then only with strong alcoholic assistance. The man with the wound knowledge stayed with him. In the morning, he told Erik, "You may take one of two choices. We can cut your leg off at the knee and hope you are not infected, or we can wash out the wound and bandage it tightly and see if you regain any freedom of movement. Either way, you will never walk normally."

"Why do these things always happen to me!?" Erik screamed. He tumbled inside to another agonizing place. His only response to pain had always been more anger. Just as he was trying to reignite his internal blaze, Nan came in—peaceful and beautiful. She kept on smiling at him, and Erik felt better because she was there. Her compassionate heart released yet another stream of tears down her face. He did not know what to say. Her caring grief caused such turmoil in him. Nan walked toward his bedside. She had heard about the two choices from the wound-knowledge man.

"If you are willing, I will walk with you through this," she spoke in a tenderness with which he was unfamiliar. Erik had no words. Small tears glistened his eyes, unsolicited.

As soon as she had said it, a messenger rushed into the room, and frantically shared that Nan's father was in trouble and she must leave immediately. She groaned for two reasons. Looking down at Erik, she clasped his hand, then with her eyes locked on his and with an intense focused voice, "I will be back," and then Nan re-whispered with stronger intention, "I will be back," and repeated her vow. She leaned over, kissed his forehead and left.

But Erik did not see or hear from her for six months. By that time, he was convinced she had been just another anguish in his tormented life, which he willingly and resolutely vectored into his hatred.

Before Erik's first full day after the fight had reached sundown, the pain in his leg and the distress of Nan's absence had become so severe, he yelled out, "Cut it off!" By the time the sun went down, he had a stub for a leg. He regretted the decision as soon as it was severed. The pain lessened over time, but he felt he was losing his mind. Nevertheless, he had been a fighter from childhood. So once again, his will to survive rose. He would beat even this. He would do it alone, without Nan, as he had always done.

He entered his chosen furnace of isolation. He would do this, as one incapacitated, all the while nurturing an evil glee to overcome it. The stub and the scars became trophies of his will power. His recovery was quicker than Mark's, but the learning process needed to conquer the stub was daunting.

Erik asked a carpenter what kind of wood was the strongest. The man told him he didn't like working with elm. So, Erik chose elm and purchased several large logs. He spent two months developing an extension for his stub. The trouble was how to fit it and then strap it to his leg.

The weeks came and went as he bloodied the stub and developed a hardened callous as the nerves deadened. At last, he had a wooden leg on his stub. His next step was to fasten a blade over the pegged limb and angle the blade slightly like a scythe. He worked in his forge, trying many angles until he made a blade he liked. Then the real work began. He trained himself rigorously on how to use his leg weapon.

The ever-present anger and his lethal motivation inspired him. Erik was energized again. He thought, *"I may be ugly, but I will still kill that man."* He was living off his revenge once more. The five had returned and worked together as he discipled them in fresh ways of violence.

When Nan came back several months later, she met an Erik she had not seen before. She looked weaker, having lost weight and her face was empty, but her eyes still bright toward him. She walked up in tears and blurted out the pain of her father's death despite her efforts to nurse him back to health. After the death of her Mom and brother, the loss of her father was doubly heavy.

Erik was in the middle of training with his leg sword when she came. She was surprised to see the pegged leg with the attached blade. She came up and tried to embrace him, but he turned away. (He remembered how he felt when Susanna had rejected him, so he wanted Nan to feel the same way.) He kept swinging his pegged sword leg as she cried out her apology and asked him to forgive her. Erik had been ignoring her as she cried. He had no tenderness for weakness. He interrupted her story, and shouted, "Where have you been?"

Nan was suddenly struck rigid in terror. The strength of his voice scared her. "Well ... uh, I was going to ..." she stammered out, and then quickly sported out the next phrases, "I was telling you my father died, and I am sorry about your leg. I am sorry I did not come back. I thought and prayed for you several times every day. I am so sorry ..."

Erik roared out, "Why do you care for me? You don't even know me! What are you trying to do to me?"

Nan lurched forward in her fatigue, able only to sob. Erik became still and began to soften a little. After a moment, he spoke softly, quietly, "You don't need to come back," but he also said it resolutely. "I will be fine." He turned away to practice with his leg.

Nan stood still ... and then her heart toward Erik lifted. After a moment, her tears stopped. Nan regained her composure and spoke in a calm but firm tone. "Erik, you are not the man you think you are. You are much better than that." She waited to let those last words sink into him. He stopped what he was doing and stood there speechless. Erik turned slowly toward her and reluctantly lifted his eyes to hers.

*"I finally see him now,"* she thought as her eyes locked with his. A degree of peace came between them. She peered into him and her gaze penetrated his pain-filled heart. Nan said, "One day, you will believe me and accept that I love you." She waited to let that approval sink in as well. "And the Lord's purpose for you ... you have not seen it yet. But when you do, I will be

167

here." She paused; then one final word, "I will be waiting for you." She walked away.

Erik continued to stand still. That moment was the first and only time he had heard the words, "I love you."

*"What do I do with that?"* His mind was a spinning wheel of emotions. *"How could anyone as nice as Nan say that ... to me? Why does she care? What did I do to make her feel that way?"* Something in his heart woke up. Something light and free and good and open.

In that light-filled moment, the five came and interrupted his wonderment. In a few seconds, Erik went back too easily to the energy of his commitment to kill Mark. This time he did not care whether it looked justified or not. He would play no games nor show any tricks. When the time came, he would go in for the kill with his knife ready and a lethal leg.

Yet, one problem still hounded his heart. Without his permission, Nan's words would come back in his dreams.

# Chapter Thirteen

# ROUND THREE—UNBELIEVABLE

The fight with Erik had occurred almost 10 months ago. A traveler brought news that Erik had been seen with a sword on his stubbed leg and was practicing hard with it. Erik was training. When Mark heard the news, he wondered, *"A sword for a stubbed leg? What would that look like?"*

Mark came to the uneasy conclusion, that although he had been wrong in his ways against Erik, he was right about the motive Erik was moving in. He recognized the threat. Mark knew then that the report about Erik's conversion was a ruse.

Mark began training again. He knew Erik would come and there would be a fight. But this time, Mark trained from a different disposition—a heart of love. Although he was wrong in the way he dealt with Erik's scheme, he was right in his underlying perception. Erik was the man behind all the trouble, but Mark had to face his many wrongs in the story.

He knew that apart from the grace of God, one of them would die this time. In Mark there was no revenge, and he was praying for God to touch Erik. Mark did not know it, but Nan was praying, too.

Erik kept dreaming about Nan's words and that she loved him. The turmoil was heavy, chaotic, and weird. *"This love stuff is hard. How can a woman as nice as Nan say that to me?"* The dreams were strange and pleasant, but they made him angry when he woke up. He was training harder to get rid of them—without any success.

Erik decided to come secretly to the fall festival. He would come on the last day dressed as an old man with baggy over clothes and a large brown robe to hide his stubbed leg and its sword. Because the air was quite brisk, his extra baggy clothes and strange gait as an older man did not draw unusual attention. He decided to attack Mark without provocation. He didn't care anymore. Mark would die, or Erik would die trying.

Mark sensed Erik might try something at the festival, but there was no sign of him. The last day came. The ladies hide and race game had been canceled until next year. The last scene of that game was still too ugly and fresh in the community's memory. The last day was closing. Those planning for an early departure were already packing the wagons for the journeys home. The king had stationed extra men as security for this festival in case there was a threat, but none appeared in the offing.

As the town was cleaning up the festival trappings, an old man approached Mark and Susanna. He was hunched over and moved like an old soldier. His head was facing the ground. As the man approached, suddenly Mark sensed him. At that moment, Erik stood to his full height, throwing off the old man garb, and spewed out his wrath. "You and I will fight, and this will be the last time; you will be carried home dead!" Mark had never heard a more confident claim.

Yet, an unusual peace came to Mark and Susanna. She

smiled, leaned up to kiss Mark, and whispered, "I love you. See you in a bit, and we will go home for dinner."

The first move Erik made was to whisk out a knife from his back and throw it like a dart right between Mark's feet into the dirt. It landed hard and penetrated the solid ground all the way to the handle. Mark did not even flinch, though he had not seen the movement until it was over. Still, he remained peaceful. He slowly withdrew his Longstreet, and Erik revealed his leg sword, gleaming like a diamond … sharp.

Mark had no idea how to fight a man with a sword for a leg. *"What would this look like?"* He remained still inside and out.

The last thing Erik saw, before he engaged Mark was Nan standing behind Susanna in the crowd. She was smiling kindly, looking concerned, and she had those clean tears running down her cheeks. She had cried often for Erik. Mad that she cared about him and more so that she loved him, Erik roared and ran forward at Mark. He moved swiftly, strangely agile with the pegged leg-sword. Although awkwardly coordinated, he was mesmerizing to watch. Suddenly, he leaped sideways and spun with his sword arching at an unexpected angle. The attack came so fast, only Mark's cat-like reflexes saved him. The tip of Erik's leg sword hissed by his face—a mere inch away.

*"He did not see that coming,"* Erik realized. *"Next time I will get him."*

Mark prepared his sword. He must learn quickly, or this would soon be over. Still, there was no anxiety. He felt at rest. Erik used numerous moves never seen before by Mark, and each time, Erik would just miss Mark's face or his side or his leg. Erik was growing frustrated with his lack of efficiency and Mark's calm countenance. Mark had not moved much at all. He adjusted only enough to avoid the leg-sword. He made no offensive maneuver, none. Erik stopped abruptly and with a single motion threw his second knife at Mark's first scar. As he released it, Erik thought, *"I have him."* But miraculously, Mark casually flipped his sword up and clinked the knife harmlessly to the ground.

Mark did it without effort. There was no anger in him or desire to attack. Mark wondered why he had no emotion, except peace and ... love? ... for Erik? Yes, that was it, his prayers for Erik had made room for a divine love. Erik was fighting to kill him, but Mark was loving him back. He was amazed at the power of God's love working in him toward a man who was trying to kill him.

Then as remarkable and ugly as the violence had been the year before, a miracle of love entered the group of people gathered around the two antagonists. Heaven opened, at least that is what the people said about that day. What occurred would be retold hundreds of times. The fight last year had been a stormy flood of bizarre and grotesque violence. It was overshadowed by a crude evil. This time, the fight was moving in a heavenly direction, at least for one of the combatants. The scene was strange, wonderful, unforgettable.

In the middle of the fight, a divine intrusion of love and praise to God arose. While Erik was attacking Mark, and Mark was only peacefully defending, with no effort to attack, a heavenly praise to God was initiated by those watching.

Into, and then out from the hearts of the community, a song of praise to the Lord began among the people. The song was unearthly. It was started softly by the lady who spoke up after the first time Mark and Erik fought. She had said, "I think we ought to pray for him," while others were speaking with harsh judging words. She was the one who started the singing.

As the praise to God rose, Erik stopped, stunned. *"What is this?"* He became still. He looked at them in wonder. "This is not church!" he yelled. He swung his leg like a scythe at Mark's legs. He missed, again. Mark was still making no effort to go on the offensive. He only deflected the rash and raging efforts of his antagonist. Every few moments, Erik would glimpse Nan's face ... her tears ... her constant, kind smile.

Erik had no idea what was going on, but he knew his resolve to kill Mark was waning; he didn't know why. Now, he was hurting more than he was angry. In an effort intended to push himself back into his rage, he swung his leg sword from as high a leap as he could muster—and missed again. He landed at an obtuse angle, precariously off balance.

Immediately, Mark lifted his sword for the first and only time in the fight. The Longstreet moved in a magnificent swoop of swift efficiency, directed toward the sword-leg. His aim was true and severed the piece of wood just below the leg's stub. He had sliced the sword from its leather strappings. Erik fell to the ground, weaponless.

Mark turned away and gave his own sword to Susanna. Then he casually walked over and knelt next to Erik, who was gasping heavily from his exertions. He laid there amazed at

Mark's kind approach. Mark spoke first and with no shame toward Erik for 20 minutes.

A divine love came over all the people, and though Erik had yelled earlier, "This is not church," it became a church for most everyone that day. Mark was giving his testimony in specific detail to Erik. He started with the time he ruined Wayne's legs, all the way up until the 40 days of prayer and the king's righteous discipline. He spoke of Erik's excellent work on his knives and his skills as a warrior. Mark finished by saying, "The king could use a man like you."

Erik was beyond surprised. This was unfathomable. Inexplicably, Erik was sensing the peace that Mark spoke of. He looked at Mark for the first time as a man and not as an enemy.

"Do you really think the king could use someone like me?"

"I do, and I will ask him if he would meet with you." Then Mark surprised Erik even more.

"Erik, I must ask you to forgive me for attacking and accusing you last year. I was wrong to do it and I was wrong in the way I did it."

Erik was swirling inside. Nan was smiling through her tears. All the people in the circle that watched were crying and this time, with no shame for either man. Then with no explanation, except for the love of God, for the first time in his life, Erik cried deep cleansing and healing sobs. No shame, just life coming into his pain-filled heart. They were heavenly tears that reached up to God from the wounds of his soul. The love of the heavenly Father was touching him. Erik had heard the words about God's love before, but now he knew this was a divine salve flowing into his pain-filled soul. It was not a human event. The One who made all things, knew all things, and held all things together was reaching into the raging storm of Erik's depths.

His voice burst forth asking Mark to forgive him for his evil plan and the deception and the attack against Susanna and the desire to kill him and ...

Mark interrupted, "We have lots to talk about and much to admit to as wrong on both sides. We can take turns repenting to God and each other. Deal?"

Erik accepted the love. He allowed the heavenly Father to pour it in. If you please, God was hugging him, and Erik hugged Him back. Then just as inexplicably and unbelievably—unless you know the power of God's love, Mark embraced Erik and they cried together.

That day, if tears had been rain, the community would have flooded. The circle stood grateful and solemn as two adversaries were reconciled to God and to one another. The Almighty God came to town that day.

That day, the tears that ran down, the cheers that cascaded off the hills, and the fears that fled away ... were mountainous.

Off to the side, and away from the crowd, stood the five. They found themselves in church that day, but not singing one note. The five were not submitting to what Erik was doing. He had trained them in harsh vengeful pathways. They had learned the lessons well and trained forcefully in what he taught them. The five were not ready to forsake the banner Erik had planted in their lives. They would carry it through to the end, even

175

though their leader had forsaken their purpose. Erik's betrayal of the goal invigorated them into a stronger ferocity. Erik may have left them, but they were determined to finish what he was not willing to conclude. They would return to confront Erik, hurt Nan, and then kill both Mark and Susanna.

King Egbert heard about what the true King had done at the festival. He smiled and cried and rejoiced.

Over the next few months, the miracles continued. Erik married Nan. Mark was the best man. Susanna, with a scarred forehead and clean heart was the matron of honor. Erik and Nan had their struggles as all marriages do. But the love, approval and support that came to them from all sides was too powerful to ignore. Erik joined a men's Bible group to learn the ways of the Lord. Their first child, a son, came two years later. They named him, Mark. Erik was also mentored by James for five years, and he turned into an even more excellent smith.

Erik taught Mark secrets of making and using a knife. Erik entered a special band of soldiers who were trained to work deeds of service throughout the realm. Erik grew to love serving people, especially younger men. He had a gift to disciple men. He would have never thought it possible. Nan was the jewel of his heart, and her love was healing him more and more as the days progressed. She was proud of her husband. She always knew that man was there, hidden under all the pain. Mark helped Erik design a peg for his stub, which was also made of elm wood and had a sword wrapped to the side of it. They became close friends for the rest of their lives.

# Chapter Fourteen

# THE POSITIONING OF A SAGE

James was declining in strength, and the entire Longstreet family had gathered. They had grown to number 57 including all the grands and greats. James still spoke with a clear voice, but he could barely walk. All knew his departure was near.

James motioned for Elizabeth to come, and he spoke tenderly into her ear. She expressed deep tender sobs. Everyone unconsciously backed away, as the two of them shared their final personal conversation—honoring the intimacy of their union. Honor is not hard to give to honorable people. Children are commanded to honor their parents, but more than that, the roots of integrity and courage are planted deeply into the soul of a child when a father and mother walk in that kind of strength with one another.

A nation's fulfillment of its' righteous destiny is inextricably connected to the health and vitality of the loving and upright parents of the next generation. If that pillar of society is eroded, a nation will not stand in mature positions. The home is where the strength of a heart is composed. If the homes and families in a nation are weak, the hearts of that people will be weak also.

> If the homes and families in a nation are weak, the hearts of that people will be weak also.

As the head of his generation held

the love of his life, everyone's eyes glistened. Glad is the man and wife who grow in that kind of love. They had finished. All stood still. Holy moments should not be rushed or quickly finalized with some cute retort, so the occasion can move on. An enduring divine silence can secure the heart into strong pe ace.

After that waiting, Elizabeth turned and asked each child to bring their spouse and children to James' side. He spent time laying his hands on them and giving each one the substance of a supernatural blessing. The experience was somber, prophetic, fascinating, divine.

There was no hurry in the house, not even a little. Every person felt and knew the peace of God coming upon them. Sometimes, the words James gave were brief and penetrating. With others, his words were filled with images like the Lord's parables. Each blessing was unique as the Spirit of God filled James' heart and mind with what was needed for that person and their generation.

As weak as James was, the Lord was providing strength for him to convey to his sons and daughters what God wanted to give into and through their life. All the members could not stand inside the house; some had gathered at the windows to hear what was proclaimed. They were all desiring to hear all that was said, not just what would be spoken to them personally. Several attentive listeners sat nearby and wrote short notes on the blessings that were spoken.

As the family had grown together before the Lord, now they stood together as the Lord was ready to receive the patriarch. At times, James' voice boomed like a trumpet blast, then he would sing sweetly to a five-year-old. The words of God stored in James' heart merged with the prayers of faith for each of these dear loved ones. He and Elizabeth had prayed day-after-day for years for all of them by name. Some of the blessings caused everyone to laugh in glad delight at the description of that child.

Then there was the profound elaboration of another one's unusual capacity to perceive the roots of trouble and how the Lord intended to position them in places of complexity and stress. The event went on for almost three hours. The Lord was smiling on the family. Nothing but love was in the air. This was not a family of regret. Their attitude did not deny genuine weaknesses. They did not use false facades as a way of life. Theirs was the legitimate vitality, gained by hearts that took God at His Word and implemented genuine steps of trust and submission to His ways. The fruit of that genuineness shows its authenticity when most others falter in the middle of opposition.

Here they were with James at death's door, and all knew death would speak in this season. Yet, the last word death was appearing to have in that moment, was just that .... only a moment. The Lord had conquered death's ability to have the final word when He rose from the dead. Everyone here knew it was true.

The sorrow of death's voice would not dominate the day. Every half hour or so, James would say, "Could we sing to our Master?" The hymns would begin among the singers of the family, and all would join in, focused and full of faith. During these singing times, James' closed eyes allowed him to gaze deeply on the Lord and His future intention for each member. James received fresh insights to bless the next family and children.

Erik and Nan were included at this holy time because they had in a few short years become part of the family. When James spoke over them, it was as if the father Erik had never known was hugging every ounce of pain and rejection from his soul. Erik spoke about that day for the rest of his life, and he smiled more from that day forward. Nan's word was as if she was a favored daughter. Nan's strength kept blossoming, and the health of the Longstreet family was bringing it out. James spoke with compassion and strength, "You are the delight of God and the unwavering faith you have shown and the love you feely give is a heritage of life for eternity! You are a warrior unto life, and your reward is great in heaven!"

Mark's family was last. Michaela, Jennifer, Zechariah, Christopher and Aaron stood, one after the other, as the blessings came with unique strength. Christopher's blessing was about his tender heart, persistent ethical clarity, ox-like strength and perceptive discerning of evil motives. "You will move forward in a straight line under the Lord's pleasure. You will win battles for the sake of those you will turn into men," James said with a sturdy smile. He also warned about evil schemes to deceive him and those he would serve, but he was promised the Lord would provide true friends and fellow soldiers.

Jennifer's word was about her vitality and prophetic clarity in discerning spirits, and it included a song about how her love for people pleased the Lord. "You are a light from heaven to all you meet." He admonished her to continue to trust as she had been, and she would see powerful displays from heaven. "Your faith is a delight to Me, says the Lord. I am so glad about you." Then James smiled and said, "I am crazy about you!" All laughed in agreement.

Zechariah's blessing revealed him as a spiritual 'dragon-slayer' with a writing gift. He was being trained by the Lord into an ambassador's status in the Kingdom. "You will find yourself in the right place at the right time, and your house will abide as a fortress into the future. I will form you into a trumpet! And your children will grow into the full stature of their purpose!"

Aaron's blessings involved having insights about how to make things right—along with deep understandings of relationships. He was instructed to continue in his firm allegiance to the Lord's ways. Biblical revelation would be a major part of his inheritance. "You are ordained to discover and unlock secrets that will heal hearts, communities, and regions."

Michaela's blessing was the hardest to comprehend and seemed to come from the invisible realm of God. James' words were heard, but not understood. He spoke casually of grand wonders in the Kingdom of God. Some of the words he used were common words, such as clouds, and trees, but interspersed were unusual usages like, 'governing shoulders' and 'prophetic horns' and 'planting the heavens' into the earth. The flow of what was being said was as if he was speaking another language. The sentences did not make sense to us, but the house filled with angelic accompaniments; everyone knew it was more of a heavenly message than an earthly one. Heaven's smile was on her.

James had finished with Michaela and then motioned for Mark and Susanna. They knelt together at the bedside. James stirred abruptly and lifted his legs to turn to them and then placing his feet, he stood. All were surprised at this exertion of physical strength. He placed his hands on their heads. The family was awed. Like a horn blasting, he was lifting his voice, and began …

"The Lord will teach you how to live in the realm of His name. The Lord will teach you the decorum of His throne room. The life of the Lord Himself will flood your days and ways. The revelation of the Lord Jesus will grow you into the royal strength of God. The Spirit of the living God will fall on you and fill the ears and eyes of your hearts with wisdom. You will discern evil workers and not be outwitted. Your battles will be against the so-called "great men" in the Bible. You will expose and overcome principalities of evil! May your steps be directed by the Lord's priorities and His eyes. May your minds be clear, your bodies strong and your voice vibrantly full of His strength until the last. Your bride is the necessary addition to make your purposes fulfilled. May your family's fruit increase to His honor until the Lord returns. May the enemies of the Lord be overcome through your lives. May you both live under His approval and may kings favor you."

James smiled and briefly hugged them. Then James whispered into Mark's ear. In the same way King Egbert had about the secret storage places. Only Mark heard him say it, "Make sure you pray and study the 'blood covenant.' It is the secret of life."

For Mark's natural ears, it was whispered, but the words his father spoke roared deeply into his spirit. Mark knew what a word from God sounded like, and these two hushed statements were trumpeted into his core. He knew it was a divine directive. The rest of the family saw the whispered act and recognized the entrance of the Spirit of God as it occurred, but they did not hear the words. They wondered of course.

James eased into Mark's strong arms and was placed back into the bed with Mark's able assistance. Elizabeth came near, and the family crowded in … as close as they could.

A song began from one of the children—it was a song of praise about the Lord's power and love. Hearts were lifted with kind gratefulness for the honor of James' life. They sang the song more than once and the words took root in their hearts. The family became more aware of the Lord's blessing than of themselves, James, or even of the earth itself. They were all lifted in spirit to the heavens, enthralled with the Lord Himself. And moments later, while all were engrossed with the Heavenly Father, their earthly father departed easily to the invisible realm … quite unnoticed.

A month after James' funeral, Mark asked King Egbert if he could go away to pray. He allowed him to go to the same cabin where he and Susanna had gone together. Mark spent 21 days crying out to the Lord. He also spent hours dedicated to the deepest listening he had known. The Lord met him there again. He took time looking at the scriptures about the blood and God's covenant priorities. Mark began to understand it is a much larger concept in the Bible. He would continue to pursue the Lord about the covenant.

And, as only the Lord can, Mark was transformed at another place of wisdom. He sensed the time away was a combination of Moses' burning bush revelation and Samuel's name being called out by the Lord for His purpose.

Mark was in his late-50s, and his years had included thousands of hours of labor, war, service, and sacrifice. Yet, after these days, he sensed he was finally positioned for his purpose in life. When Sir John, his trainer for the Blue Guard, had died years earlier, he knew the mentoring, which had been provided to him was now a debt he owed to all that he could mentor. Now, with his father's passing, the weight of the privilege of being a disciple-maker came upon him and felt like a heavy robe.

Two months after he returned from this 21 days of prayer, King Egbert called him to the castle. When Mark arrived in the throne room, Jonathan, the king's son, was also in the throne room. Egbert motioned Mark to come close and sit with them at a table to one side of the throne.

The two men listened as the king relayed his plan for the transfer of power to his son. He wanted Mark to hear it. The recorder was there, but he was only a hearing writer. The recorder was forbidden to ever speak what was said in the throne room. Any breach of throne room secrets was grounds for immediate execution, so there was no threat of the recorder betraying the king's trust. If anyone was trusted, it was the recorder.

The words heard by those men that day were marvelous and intimidating. True kings move in wisdoms most people cannot fathom. The details and impact are far-reaching along with the multi-faceted considerations connected to any decision. The wisdom of a great heart and a fearless willingness to delve into stormy complexities is a great challenge.

The king surprised Mark once more when he asked him to serve as Jonathan's chief counselor. Jonathan had already given his approval to that choice. If Mark accepted, he would be moving into the very core of the king's agenda. If he thought their life had been dominated by the king's will before, it would be utterly consumed by the king's will now, and the king's will alone. Mark said, "Yes." A wise person would not say no to the will of the king.

Within two weeks, King Egbert died. Mark's leaders were passing to their reward. The gap he felt by these deaths produced an aloneness in him that lasted for two years. Several times, during those two years when he was considering a decision, he would think, *"I will speak with my father,"* only to realize a moment later, *"I cannot talk to him."*

The chasm in his interior never fully went away. The gap was one only the Lord could fill up, and Mark would ask Him to fill it over and over as he moved forward.

# POSTSCRIPT

Galvin, Edward and Mark's bond of brotherhood was solid as a rock. They knew how each other would act in battle, as well as being intimately acquainted with each other's weaknesses and strengths. They loved each other and were each willing to die for the other without hesitation. In fact, they all had saved the life of the other two more than once.

As stated in the first part of our story, this trio experienced a perfect joining of love and friendship. This kind of relationship is rare, but when it is formed, it produces multiple blessings. In the third and final volume of this story, we will witness the most wonderful and difficult events of their lives. We will discover that righteous living, provided by the grace of God, does not exempt us from trouble. But it does establish us in and on a rock. And that rock is not moved by the storms of life.

In the last story of our series, the Vikings will come back with unprecedented pressures, and they are confederated with a treasonous band. Since King Egbert and James have departed, death continues to come in stunning new ways and overwhelms Mark. It becomes a sorrow, which threatens every strength he has moved in.

The five trained by Erik also rise, with an enraged unity against Mark, Erik, and King Jonathan. These five sons of Baal will fulfill their evil dream or die. Old friends return at the right moment to bring miraculous help against those who are intensified in accomplishing and going beyond Erik's plan.

Friend and foe die the day they initiate their wicked work. The trio of Mark, Galvin and Edward will also have one last stand where they are hopelessly surrounded.

# COMING SOON ...

## FORGED IN FIRE
## —THE LONGSTREET—
### The Complexities of a Sage

## Vol. 3

# INTRODUCTION

# THE SECRET EXPOSED:
# A SCHEME TO STEAL

A sailor on Captain Charles' ship was at Monkwearmout. He had helped unload and load the boxes of dirt from Japan when James, Mark and David had come to pick it up. Captain Charles had understood the need for discretion and promised to keep the family secret unspoken. But, decades of family strength cannot be gained or maintained by an outsider in a moment. Captain Charles did not betray their confidence intentionally, but he was innocently unguarded two years later.

His boat and its sailors were on a journey in the North Sea when a sturdy storm erupted, reminding them of the storms they had been through before. They talked in the galley about those previous storms at dinner. They were in the bowels of the boat. The storm when they carried the 14 boxes of dirt was mentioned. "That was an especially harsh one, where we almost lost the ship, except for the ballast provided by the special dirt from Japan for swords that kept us upright," said the Captain.

One of the more alert sailors noted the Captain's emphasis on special dirt. He was always looking for a way to obtain benefits without regard for ethical limitations and found the Captain's comments intriguing. In other words, he was a thief.

In a disinterested tone to veil his intent, he asked, "Captain, you have served well in many storms. Do you think that storm with the boxes of dirt (he avoided using the word special on purpose, not wanting the Captain to know he heard the emphasis the Captain had put on it) may have been the worst storm of your career?"

The Captain did not discern his motives and answered, without any alertness, "Yes, it was one of the worst ones, but maybe the one where we lost three men due to the pitching of the boat was the worst one."

Offhandedly, the sailor replied, "I guess what you said is true, maybe that was special dirt, since it saved our lives when it supplied the needed extra ballast."

Still unaware, the Captain divulged the secret, "No, that dirt was special because it is used to make swords that are unusually strong. Those swords are highly valuable. The dirt is prized for the swords it makes for kings."

The sailor wisely and casually responded, "Oh," and shifted the topic, away from the dirt. "Captain, do you think we will have another storm tomorrow?"

"There are always storms. They come when they come. We must be prepared for them." He did not know he had baited the heart of a greedy man. That greedy man launched a plan that very night. The secret being revealed was a seed into the thieving soil of his heart.

For three months, the sailor investigated the information regarding the special dirt. He spoke to the men who worked at the port. One day, he found someone who had known the

Japanese man who brought the boxes of dirt. Then, four months later, he was introduced to that man from Japan and posed as a friend of Mark's. (In his searching for information over the months, he discovered tidbits of the story about the large swordsmith and got Mark's name from a storekeeper near the wharf. He had been composing a deceitful tale for months. He used it when he found the merchant from Japan.)

The story was practiced and finely honed. He displayed himself with ease and the merchant suspected nothing. He asked about the secrets of the dirt and heard the truth about its key ingredients in creating the samurai sword's unique capabilities. His greedy eyes shone with anticipated wealth. The scheme matured in his covetous heart. He invested his life in the plot to steal the dirt. He would meet Mark with a team formed and ready to make the heist. He paid the team a lot less than the dirt was worth. Its' true value he kept to himself.

Mark had no idea the family secret had been uncovered until it was too late.

# ABOUT THE AUTHOR

Michael Massa is passionately focused on the Word and work of the Lord Jesus. He has served in ministry for over 45 years, and his experience includes travel to 24 nations.

He is a pastor, teacher, author, songwriter, the glad husband to Nancy and a father to their 4 adult children and 4 'grands.

To contact Michael, go to:

mikemassa77@gmail.com